THE SCARPACCI FILES

J. J. CANIGLIA

ARPress

ARPress
45 Dan Road Suite 36
Canton MA 02021

Hotline: 1(800) 220-7660
Fax: 1(855) 752-6001

Ordering Information:
Quantity sales. Special discounts are available on quantity purchases by corporations, associations, and others. For details, contact the publisher at the address above.

Printed in the United States of America.

ISBN-13:   Paperback   979-8-89389-637-4
           Hardback   979-8-89389-638-1
           eBook   979-8-89389-639-8

Library of Congress Control Number: 2024921307

This book, my first book, is dedicated to my children. Gino, Vinnie, Arabella, and Sarafina, you four are the most important people in my life, and I do this for you. I do this in hopes of making something of myself, for you. I do this in hopes of leaving something behind, even if it is just my name on paper. I do this to make you proud.

*If an injury has to be done to a man it should be so
severe that his vengeance need not be feared.*

—*Niccolo Machiavelli*

*Vengeance is in my heart, death in my hand, blood
and revenge are hammering in my head.*

—*William Shakespeare*

Contents

Prologue

S THE METAL door slams shut against the metal frame, the silence explodes with a ferocious *CLANG* from behind him. Without a flinch, he continues to walk away. His eyes stay fixating on something in front of him. People all around him are expressing their goodbyes, but they remain unheard. He concentrates on the hallway he is walking down, it appears longer and darker than it did the first time he walked it.

He is more nervous now, with his final walk, than he was with his first trip upon it. With each step his heart trembles. It seems as if being released from an institution is almost as bad as being admitted to one. He knows not what to expect as he crosses to the other side of that gate, though he knows what *must* be done. As he approached the end of the hall, he turns to his right and enters a large corridor. There are spider webs hanging in every corner, mold growing in every dark nook and cranny. The concrete walls had cracks as numerous as the prisoners that they held back, some were even beginning to crumble in areas. As he approaches the end of the corridor, he glances out of an open door.

The sun shines brightly as its rays crash through the door. Right above it, a sign hanged. His eyes, squinting from the sun, open a little as they lift upwards towards this sign. He can clearly see what is in front of him, but is this the path that he truly wants to follow? This path has been forged for him already, not by fate, nor destiny, but by his own doing. The past decade has been created by his own hand. His brother and himself can only go one way. Either onwards, the way that they have been going, or to start all over and forget everything that has already happened.

The latter seems to be the best way. A real-life with a real job, a wife, maybe some kids. As he stares at the sign, he knows that a real-life for him is out of the question. There was only one girl in his life that he ever really loved, but he hasn't heard from her in years. Her name, Arabella. Arabella from Palermo. Arabella, the beautiful Sicilian girl from down the street. The two of them met shortly after arriving in the city. They almost lived the cliché story of guy meets girl, love at first sight sort of thing. She had eyes that were so blue, bluer than the sea that crashed upon the rocks off the Sicilian shores. Her eyes reminded him of home, not home in Omaha, or New York, but Carlentini, Sicily.

When he was given this new concrete home, he was taken from his family, and from Arabella. She promised to always love him and swore that they would be together again at some point. In the beginning, she wrote two or three letters every week expressing her love and sorrow at being away from him. Eventually, the letters dwindled, and the content became numb. The love loss was obvious more and more with each letter. There were no more, *I love you's*, no more, *you are missed*. These letters became routine, they became a habit, mostly just formalities. *Hi, how are you, things here are fine*, just checking to make sure that you're not dead kind of letters.

The outgoing letters were of a mirrored image, though his feelings were not. He didn't want to let on that his love for her was still just as strong knowing that she had obviously moved on. He feels as if men should always remain strong, and put up a front, even if it means losing her. To express his feelings would show sensitivity. A sort of sensitivity that one could consider a weakness and a man in his position cannot afford to show any weakness. Instead of reminding her and himself how he feels, he let her go. He let her go, free to live her life without any tie-downs or distractions on his part. Even still, his love for Arabella will always remain, even when hers for him does not.

No… no wife and family for him, that's not in his cards. His fate was sealed that one bloody night that his father was ripped from this world. His fate was delivered upon him by the hands of evil, and evil cannot truly be erased without fighting back with equal amounts of evil, if not more. He squints his eyes once more to look through the blinding rays, out through the door. Beyond the door were armed guards, and beyond them was a rather large fence and gate. Even further, his brother stood, leaning up against his car and smiling.

Yano looks back up at the sign. *Exit*. Exit this life and start a new, or, exit this prison and continue what needs to be continued. Yano smiles as his head tilts back down toward his brother, Gino, and he walks through the door. Yano knows exactly from what path his life must not veer.

In the New World

IN THE YEAR 1908, the little town of Omaha is on the verge of change, change so drastic that it will shake the town to its very core, the sort of change that you never know you want until years after it happens. On the north Atlantic sailed the ships of immigrants from Sicily to the new world. The ships docked at the shores of Ellis Island. From one of those ships walked out Enzo and Fina Scarpacci (scar-pah-chee). A Sicilian couple, that had grown ever so tired of the constant struggles of everyday life in such a beautiful but very poor country, managed the treacherous waters and brought their children to America. To America, they came for opportunity, a place in which the streets were paved with gold, or so they were told.

After arriving at Ellis Island and going through all their formalities with entering the country, the family boarded a train to their new home. After a few days of traveling aboard the train, they finally pulled into the station in Omaha Nebraska. There was already a little Italy neighborhood building itself up. Many houses were already built and occupied, others still in the progress of being built. More and more immigrants were flooding into America every day and they had to have places to live, so construction was a good business to be in.

Enzo was able to find work as a stonemason rather quickly, as an immigrant with no money, he was willing to do just about anything. The work was backbreaking and had long hours along with minimal pay, but money had to be made. Fina found work as a nurse in a small clinic near the railroad. She would administer shots and other aid to other immigrants coming to the city. Some were starving and needed to be fed. No matter what the need, Fina was there to help, also for next to nothing wages.

The two immigrants had a couple of children tagging along with them across the world. From Sicily to America also came three little Scarpaccis. The eldest child, a son, Yano. He was 15 years old which makes him old enough to sit at home with the other two while their parents were at work. The second child, Gino, was 12. He was a strong-willed, knuckleheaded, kind of boy. Lastly came Rosaria. She was only seven but already too smart for her age. She was already learning math, reading, and writing, and coming from a poor country with minimal schooling available, this was impressive.

Enzo goes to work every day, fifteen-hour days, and was still having trouble paying their bills. Fina's weekly salary was not much help, especially with the extra bills that the new homelands came with. There was an organization running the neighborhood, it was a secret organization but everyone knew of them. Known as the Black Hand, this organization ran the neighborhood through fear. Extortion was their main racket as the neighborhood businesses were forced into paying them for protection. The payments were too high and most businesses could not afford it. The small business would eventually go away, so the Black Hand began extorting civilians as well. They were forced to pay protection, sort of a home owner's insurance.

Enzo was one of the neighborly civilians that was forced into this payment plan. He would come home almost crying some nights because he knew that their new life was not going to be a good one if they were forced to continue with these payments. How could anyone make a living when they are forced to give most of their income away? It just isn't fair he thought. Why won't someone step up and stop this? Enzo is not the type to do this. He was five foot six and just over one hundred thirty-five pounds. He didn't have an ounce of fat nor muscle on his entire body, purely skin and bones, he was. Imagine a scrawny, average-sized man, trying to stand up for himself to an entire organization with absolutely no backing. The entire neighborhood felt the same as Enzo, but the men were all spineless. They were law-abiding citizens, they wanted good honest work with good honest lives. Going up against men with guns was not in any of their styles, *it's just not in good taste*, as Enzo would put it.

Throughout the neighborhood, this organization was known, but beyond all others, one name stood out, Gianni Spilotti. Gianni was the main enforcer in this part of the neighborhood. The man was a beast, standing almost six feet tall and weighing well over two hundred fifty pounds. His size alone intimidated people. His eyes, his eyes were dark, not so much in color but in feeling. When the man would glance across the room you could feel the fear spread from person to person. He gave off such an aura of hatred and despair that would stink up an entire city block around him. He was a soulless man and he wasn't trying to hide the fact.

Rumors get started when people are afraid of something, or just don't like someone. Well, in Gianni's case, people were both afraid and full of dislike, so rumors began. These could have been true stories but as far as most people knew, they were only rumors. One story, in particular, Gianni once cut the fingers from a women's hand because her husband refused to pay. The story says that the man refused four times and his wife lost four fingers because of it. When he finally decided to pay, the wife was let go, bleeding from four bloody, infected holes where her fingers once were, as she walked herself to the hospital. Her husband, however, was not so lucky. The story says that after he collected the enforcer's money, the man then had his eyes removed from his face.

Gianni did not use a knife, but a spoon, and he did it in such a gentle way that the man did not die. He just kind of sat there, his head pointing upwards but still only seeing the floor as his eyeballs dangled downwards from their sockets. Causing injury to the eye is a symbol of greed, the man tried to stop paying the organization. They saw this as a sort of greed and decided to send a message to the neighborhood. To the Black Hand, they saw this message as pay for our protection or protect yourself against us. Though the neighborhood saw this message as, what is ours is ours, and what is yours is also ours.

Enzo didn't pay much attention to these rumors, though he was afraid of him. He was afraid because he knew what the Black Hand was capable of doing. He does not fear for himself but for the safety of his wife and children. Enzo was being forced to pay twenty-five dollars a month which was almost his entire earnings. His family suffered for it, but in order to keep them safe, he never missed a payment. He and his wife, Fina, were both forced to work long backbreaking hours to make up for the loss, so they were not home with the children as much as they should have been.

When their parents were away at work, Yano would leave his sister with Gino and sneak outside and watch the neighborhood kids play. Yano was attracted to the life of the neighborhood street gang, the Two Kingdom Boys. They took their name from the kingdom of Two Sicilies. Two Sicilies was an era in time from 1815 to 1860. The island of Sicily, as well as the southern mainland of Italy, were as one. Sicily one was the island and Sicily two was the mainland, however, the Kingdom of Sardinia annexed one of the Sicilies and it became the Kingdom of Italy in 1861. The boys used this name to show that even though the two Sicilies were now separate, they were still united by blood and history as one people. Yano was instantly drawn to this life of thuggery and lawlessness. How someone could live without fear of punishment was inconceivable to most but exciting to him.

Yano ran into one of these boys on his way home from school one day. The boy was upset that Yano didn't show him the respect in which he felt he deserved. A few other boys from the gang approached and Yano knew that he was in for some trouble. Being a hard-headed young boy that he was, he stood his ground to all four of the others. The boys began shoving him back and forth, Yano closed his hand into a fist and without aiming, swung it as hard as he could at the first boy. His knuckles made a loud slapping noise as they connected with the boy's cheek. The boy fell to the floor, this is when the fists started flying from all directions.

The three boys were pummeling Yano hard, though he did not fall down. Yano's face began to swell above his eyes, the bridge of his nose cracked open, blood was pouring from both nostrils and his lower lip. Yano still would not fall. His knees began to feel weak, and he wanted to sit and rest, but he had to stand his ground. He continued to throw his fists around in circles wildly until one more of the boys was knocked to the ground. As he fell, Yano's fist slammed into another boy's face with such fierce impact his tooth flew from his mouth. This boy stumbled back but did not fall. He regained his composure and yelled for the other boys to stop.

As the boys all stood there, bloody and tired, they studied Yano. What a monster this kid could potentially be for them. He has the strength of a wounded lion. The type of strength that knows it is outnumbered but refuses to die, refuses to give up, and refuses to quit.

A man willing to die on his feet instead of live on his knees is the kind of man they all wished to be.

From across the street, on her porch, sat a girl watching the entire thing. She also studied Yano with such disbelief that he could stand for so long and take such a beating without hitting his knees once. As she watched, the boys seemed to almost accept Yano as one of their own, they nodded at him and walked away.

"Hey, are you ok?" yelled the girl.

Yano looked over at the girl and was in shock. He had to rub the blood from his eyes to make sure what he was seeing was true. This was the most beautiful girl that Yano had ever seen.

"I'll be alright".

"You sure? You don't look alright."

Yano starred at her with a look in his eyes that he has never had before. He walked over to the girl and began to talk to her.

"Why are you so worried about me?" he asked.

"Well, look at ya"

"Ya but didn't you see them also? I only look this bad because there were four of them." Yano snickered a little bit as he acted tough for the girl.

"I am not sure if you're that conceited, or just dumb."

"And what do you mean by that?" Yano asked persistently. The girl began to talk and as she did, Yano could tell that she was educated. She was not from the same school that he went to. No, her father had money. She was homeschooled by the finest tutors. Her name is Arabella. Her eyes were as blue as the ocean, and her hair was long and dark. She had tan skin and was the most beautiful girl Yano had ever seen. Not just Yano, but all of the neighborhood boys were after her. Arabella was an Italian supermodel in their eyes, the daughter of a goddess.

Yano watches as her mouth moves, forming the words of their native language with perfection. Love, at first sight, can be real, and Yano is finding this out first hand. How can America get any better, he thought.

As the thought of marriage and long-lasting life with this girl ran through his head, he felt as if he were on top of the world. Yano felt as of now he was in love and nothing could bring him down. What he didn't know was that the new world was not so much different than the old country. Death comes for us all. The things that were upcoming for the next few days would quickly yank Yano's head out of the clouds.

Am I the Sun?

ONE YEAR, ALMOST to the day, that the Scarpacci family had moved to America, they still were not seeing the riches that they were once promised back in Sicily. The streets are paved with gold they were told, yet when they arrived here in Omaha they saw that the streets were not paved at all. They were simply dirt roads with horse prints and wagon tracks on them. Enzo was walking home and was looking at these roads, he smiled thinking that he couldn't believe that they were tricking so many immigrants to come here and pave these roads for them. It was a sad, yet funny thought. He then realized that it was actually working. Immigrants were flooding these unpaved streets looking for work and ended up as road pavers. He smiled and let out a little laugh as he continued his walk home. As he was walking, a man ran up from behind him and pushed him. Enzo's back was shoved inward and it was as if his feet and head didn't move until his stomach could come forward no more. As his torso snapped forward, he fell to the ground and began to roll along the dirt.

Enzo rolled on to his side and looked up at his assailant. Just as his head turned towards the man, his foot came flying at Enzo's face and hit him with such an impact that flipped his body over one hundred and eighty degrees. Enzo landed back in the dirt, his eyes were rolling around in his head, he could not see straight. As he lay there on his stomach, frantically trying to get his vision back, his arms were shaking and reaching out to grasp onto anything that would help stabilize his body. Before he could get his mind back to a whole, another foot came in. This time in a downward stomping motion and hit Enzo again in the face. His face now lay motionless in the dirt.

Laughing, the man stood above Enzo, not moving at all. Enzo reached into his pocket and the man quickly grabbed him by the neck, "NO!" he screamed.

"Don't hurt me anymore! Please! I have money, please take it and leave me be!"

The man continued to laugh as he muttered, "Oh I already planned on it." Enzo pulls out all of his money and drops it on the street. Along with the gold pocket watch that his father had given him when he left for America. Enzo pleaded with the man to spare his life.

"I have a family" Enzo mumbled.

"So do I" the man replied as he shrugged his shoulders as if to say that he doesn't care. He then began to chuckle a little more and pulled out a gun. Enzo was still down, moving around, but still down. He began to get up, now on his hands and knees but still, face pointing downward.

"I have not seen your face sir, and I cannot describe you to the police. I have no gun of my own nor any outlaw courage, so revenge from me will never come. Please, you have nothing to worry about by letting me go. Please do not kill me."

The man demanded more money, as Enzo told him that there was no more to be given, the man became angry. The laughing had now stopped. It was no longer funny to the man with the gun. He realizes now that the few dollars that Enzo had, along with the watch, was not even worth the time of this robbery. The man turned the pistol around so that the barrel was in his hand. He swung his arm downward and hit Enzo with the handle in the back of the head. Enzo's body collapsed. He laid on the road, now completely still. The fight was about gone from his body. He rolled over and looked up at the sky.

Enzo saw a blurry cloud as his face and eyes were filled with blood. He saw the sun begin to hide behind the clouds as the sky gradually became a dark grey. The man was still speaking to Enzo, but he couldn't hear anything. His attention was fixed on the sun. I was a happy man walking home today, he thought. Until this man appeared, my day was full of sunshine. Like the sun I ran and hid. I could've gotten up and tried to fight back, but instead, I fell to my knees and cowardly begged. The sun saw a dark cloud and quickly ran behind the other clouds. Will this one dark cloud put out the warmth, will it end the brightness that the sun shines on the Earth? Why is it afraid? Why am I afraid? Am I the sun? This man is surely going to kill me. I have known it the entire time. Why don't I run? Why do I not fight for my life? Why does the sun not fight through the darkness? Why can I not stop fearing death when death is imminent? Can I be brave enough to stand up and at least try? Surely the sun's brightness could defeat the little dark cloud.

As Enzo lay there staring at the sky and thinking, the sun never came back out to fight off the darkness. It only becomes darker and started to rain. I *am* the sun, Enzo thought again with disappointment. A loud crashing noise awoke Enzo from this trance that he had been in. It was the sound of a gunshot. The man was yelling at Enzo now. As Enzo looked over at the man and got his first glimpse of who was doing this to him, he recognizes him. As he is about to ask why; the man slams the cold steel of the pistol into Enzo's forehead. He began to beat him with the weapon repeatedly. The only thing Enzo could do now is hope for a misfire that would end with the man accidentally shooting himself.

The man finally stopped beating Enzo and stood towering above him. He pointed the weapon at Enzo's forehead. Enzo began to cry. The man couldn't tell though, his face already soaked from blood and rain, but a lone tear fell from Enzo's eye as he finally realized that this was the end. He would never see his beautiful wife anymore, nor would he be there to help his boys grow into men. Little Rosaria would grow up without a father, being so young her memories of Enzo would quickly fade. His wife would never again fall into his arms as they both came home from a long day's work, had a family dinner, and then lay in bed together expressing their love, ready to do it all over again in the morning.

A memory of days past ran through Enzo's mind, a day at the beach in Carlentini. He could see his beautiful children playing in the ocean. The kids splashing in the water and jumping around laughing as the waves came crashing in on top of them, knocking them down and pulling them underneath. Fina was lying on the hot sand collecting the rays from the sun trying to tan her already tan Sicilian skin while Rosaria builds sandcastles next to her. Enzo was picking up Yano and throwing him gently into the deeper water and watching him sink and then jump back above the water, laughing and screaming, "Do it again Dad, do it again!"

One more loud noise, and then Enzo could see nothing. The bullet from the man's pistol exited the barrel only to enter Enzo's head ending any and all thoughts of his forever. The man took a few steps backward, looked at Enzo, and mumbled, "You should've had more money" before running off into the alley. The man seemed upset as if killing Enzo was not his Original plan. He seemed as if he went into a state of instant remorse.

Across the dirt road was an old house. Inside this old house was an older man in his mid-forties. This man had lived in this neighborhood since it first began the construction phase. His house was one of the first to be built here and he knew how the neighborhood worked. Stay out of the Black Hand's way and mind your business. If something does not concern you, then you should not concern yourself with it. In this case, this man, Dino Ganapini, did exactly that. When the first gunshot rang out, he was startled. He walked to his window and watched the rest of the event unfold. He was most likely not the only neighbor to do so.

Dino was a man of principle. He watched the event happen and stayed out of the way, though he never felt good about how it happened. He felt as if he should help but knew that if he did, then who would be there to help him. He watched as Enzo lay there bleeding in the mud pleading for his life. He watched as the man struck Enzo down in such a cowardly way for only a few dollars. Dino thought to himself, how could a man laugh hysterically while committing such a crime, and seem as if he felt bad once it was over. How could a human being's emotions switch that fast, that easy? How could this man, so guiltlessly, gun down a human life in the street like a horse with a broken leg?

Dino was reassured as he watched this man turn and run away into the alley that some people are ruthless and uncaring about anything but themselves, then wondered if they even really care about themselves. Do they have even the capacity to fear for their own safety? This angered Dino, he wants to do something about it, but what? His sons were only 16 and 13 years old, what sort of vengeance could be handed out by the hands of a dead man's children? Any chance of change that this neighborhood will ever hold will only be for the worse if something isn't done, someone has to do something.

Enzo's funeral service was a few days later. He had only lived a few blocks from the Scarpacci residence and even though he was never formally introduced to any of them, he went to pay his respects. The front door leads directly into the living room, which was filled with chairs. Off to the left, there was an archway leading into the dining area and the kitchen right beyond that. The dining area had a few tables in which people sat trays of food. There at the front of the living room, in front of all of the chairs, was a table. This table held the casket with Enzo. A line of people stood in front of it waiting to say their goodbyes. As each person approached the table, they would either kneel and say a prayer or just stand there and do the sign of the cross. In the name of the father, the son, and the holy spirit could be heard over and over. As Dino walked into the Scarpacci house he saw Fina off in the corner of the dining room, crying and holding her daughter. Gino was sitting in a chair, just staring off into space with a few tears rolling down his cheeks. Yano was not visible.

Arabella walked into the house, she was in tears. Gino looked at her and nodded, she then proceeded to head straight upstairs. Yano must be upstairs as well, Dino thought. In his bedroom, away from all of these people. Yano and Arabella had grown so close, so fast, that they were never apart from one another. Yano was not allowed at her house because of her dad, who he has never met, but Arabella would come over to his house all of the time. They would take walks together and go down to the river and have picnics, and just lay there for hours talking and escaping the neighborhood.

As Arabella left the room, Dino said paid his respects. He put his hand on Gino's shoulder. As Gino looked up at him he heard, "I am sorry for your loss, kid. Maybe someday I can help you out." He then walked away leaving Gino completely stumped. Gino had no clue who this man even was, nor what the words he spoke were supposed to mean. He just stares blankly as Dino walks out of his house.

Yano didn't stay as calm as Gino. When he heard the news that his father had been murdered, his spirits broke. It was as if his entire world had begun to crumble. He is sixteen years old and his father was his best friend at this time in his life, and now he is gone.

School suffered for Yano, he decided that he wasn't going to continue attending. He is the man of the house now and he cannot waste his time in a classroom, he needs to help his mother. He started to hang around with the Two Kingdom Boys a lot more, looking for some fast cash, and maybe a little rebellion.

One day, as Yano was leaving the grocery store, he ran into Dino. Dino had tried to speak with him once before but it didn't go too well. Yano was not too welcoming when it came to conversing with people he does not know well. This time Dino was a bit more adamant about it. They had a long conversation about how things work in life for a man and about the ways of the neighborhood. He also spoke of how Yano needs to quit hanging with the gang so much. Yano tried to blow off the conversation at this point.

"The only way you're going to help your mom is by going back to school," Dino said.

"Oh Ya? What do you know about anything?"

"I know that your father would not like the path that you are choosing for yourself!"

Yano tries to brush it off and turns to walk away. To him, Dino doesn't know what he is talking about. After all, he didn't even know his father.

"It's not just yourself boy! You're setting your brother down a path of destruction as well!"

Yano stopped walking. He stares blankly straight ahead as if confused by what he sees, though what he sees is not what is confusing him.

"That's right!" Dino says, "Do you honestly think that Gino isn't a witness to the destructive path that you have chosen? Do you think that he isn't going to follow you? His big brother?"

Yano turns to look at Dino,

"And what am I supposed to do about that? I am not his boss, his way of life is not my choice!"

"No, it's not your choice! But it *is* your responsibility. You are his older brother and it is now and will *always* be your responsibility to look after him. He will follow you to the end of the world and back Yano. You need to wake up and realize that your actions will affect more than just yourself."

Dino's words hit Yano and he starts to understand what he is talking about. He begins to realize that maybe Dino is not trying to be disrespectful but trying to simply put Yano back in the place where he needs to be. He needs to get back to school, start looking after his brother and sister more. Helping out around the house will help his mother out but so would getting a legitimate job. His and Arabella's togetherness has suffered some in the past weeks since his father died as well. Getting his life back to the way it was is what he needs to do.

Enzo is no longer here in this world. Yano no longer has a father to help him out when he needs it. How can he go back to the way things used to be when things can never go back? Enzo cannot be brought back, their pain can never be erased. There is no point in pretending. The only thing that he can do now is to look after Gino, no matter what path they each choose.

Dino could tell that his words were getting through to Yano. He had this look on his face as if he were deep in thought. He decided to break Yano's thought bubbles and begin talking again.

"Hey kid, I am not trying to force you to do anything," he started "I just want to help get you back to where you need to be. With your dad gone now, you need someone to look after you. I live only a few minutes away from you and I have no problems with speaking with you if you ever need anything. Just knock on my door, I will always answer."

Yano nods his head and walks away. Dino's words hit home, but they do not fully sink in. It only takes a few more weeks and Yano brings his brother in on the burglary ring that he had started. Breaking into stores at night and robbing them to help their mother pay bills as well as the Black Hand. He originally wanted to do as Dino said and keep his brother on a clean path, but the more he thought about it the less that made sense.

Yano and his friend Angelo were beginning this crime ring and splitting everything fifty percent. However, they both knew that they needed another guy to be the lookout guy. Instead of bringing in another fellow gang member, Yano brought in Gino. This way it does split profits a little more but it is giving them two-thirds of the profit instead of fifty percent to take home to Fina. Without Gino, Yano would lose money and only bring home thirty-three percent. Yano didn't want to bring in his brother but he didn't want to lose the money. Also, Gino was so excited to spend some time with the big brother that he lost when their father died. Yano strayed so far from home since Enzo's incident, that Gino never really got to see him anymore.

This burglary ring went on for close to a year before the Black Hand started getting wise to it. The people were running out of savings to pay them and business began to shut down. Some were beginning to be put out of business as well. Mysterious fires and explosions began happening as the Black Hand's money started to dwindle. Yano knew that this racket was just about over for them. He did not like knowing that people were getting hurt, losing their businesses, and even killed in one instance, because of them.

Yano wanted to walk away from this job and look for other means of income, however, Angelo talked him out of it. Angelo tried to explain to Yano that they would switch to a different neighborhood. The black community was only a few blocks down the road and they didn't have any organization taking from them. There were some young black men that would also go around and rob their neighborhood stores, but no true threat like the Black Hand in their neighborhood.

Yano still being affected by the loss of his father is in no way looking to get out of a rebellious lifestyle. Gino, who was a few years younger than Yano, learned to cope with his father's death easier. Maybe because he still had an older brother to look up to whereas Yano did not. Gino was willing to give it up, but he liked the excitement that it brought. He loved being so close to his brother and would go anywhere that Yano did, so whatever Yano decided, he would be fine with. Gino has no respect for authority and this trait was learned. He had been watching Yano since Enzo died and he learned this particular trait. Anything Yano did, Gino would always be right by his side.

Angelo Patrucco

NGELO PATRUCCO WAS a boy from the neighborhood. He
was the same age as Yano, and their families both come from the
same town in Sicily. Angelo, or Angie, as they called him at times,
was one of the smartest kids who ran with the Kingdom Boys. Yano
was drawn to him not only because they were both from Carlentini, but
due to his smarts. The kid had a knack for criminal tendencies, but he
was smart about how he went about doing them. He is not one of those
shoot first talk second types of kids, and Yano respected that.

Most people are taught the difference between what is right, and
what is wrong, as children. Because of this, most people also can tell
what is good and what is evil. Angie was one of those children, and he
used this as if it were his superpower. When it came time to do illegal
activities, Angie had no problem with stepping back and looking at the
picture as a whole. Whereas most people would rush right in, Angie was
there weighing risk vs reward, every time. He was one of the smartest
kids Yano had ever met. Before every job, Angelo would check it out,
review all facts, and then make a judgment call. Yano and Gino both
listened to anything he said throughout every job that the three pulled
together.

As the months slowly turn into years, the boys have pulled hundreds of robberies. Enough to keep Fina working comfortably and not having to stress over paying bills. Her hours were even able to be cut back, Yano didn't want her to have to work so many hours per day. After all, who would look after Rosaria? As Fina began working regular hours, she didn't consider asking where the money was coming from, not one time. Of course, she was curious and worried about her boys, but she was also tired. She had been working such long hours for so long now and it was beginning to take a toll on her. The Black Hand were also getting paid on time every month. Gianni Spilotti would make his way to his collection point and Yano would be there to greet him monthly, like clockwork.

As Yano was making his monthly payment, Gianni made a comment that he did not care for.

"This is the job of a man, not a little boy. What sort of father leaves his young son to provide for the family?"

As he makes his comment, then releases a small snicker under his breath, Yano looks up at him. He wants to respond, but how? What does Yano say to a man like this? The man is easily four times his size, and ready to kill at the drop of a dime. Also, he could kill in public, with witnesses, and not get in trouble. He is Black Hand. This comes with certain benefits.

"He was murdered," Yano said. "It's not as if he was a bum who ran out on us, he was murdered."

"Well, maybe he should've acted like a man and protected himself a little better. Maybe then he would still be here for you. Maybe then he would still be here for his pretty little wife." Gianni started to laugh again and finished with, "How is your mother anyway? Does she need me to come by for a visit?"

Yano was infuriated now. As he thought about pulling his blade from his boot and sticking it in Gianni's jugular, he began to shake. Yano became so angry that a single tear began to form in the corner of his eye, his arms were shaking, he wanted to jump and strangle the life from this man. Angelo quickly came over and grabbed Yano and pulled him away.

"C' mon Yano, you can't do this right now," Angie said.

"Then when Ang? When? You find me a time that I *can* do it and you let me know!"

Yano walks away so angry and leaves Angie and Gino behind. Gino tries to catch up to his brother but Angelo grabs his arm, "No, Gino. Leave him be, he needs time to cool off, and we need time to come up with a plan."

Angie gets Yano pulled back and beginning to calm down as they walk through the neighborhood.

"Let's go see Arabella. When was the last time you saw her?"

"I was there the other day," Yano replied. "Her father doesn't like her speaking with boys though. I have to leave when he is on his way home."

"What time is that?"

"Usually around nine o'clock."

"Well shit, we got plenty of time. It's only a quarter to seven right now. Let's go."

Yano was in love with Arabella but he didn't like to go see her when he felt this way. He didn't want to seem as if he were mad at her, but he knew why Ang wanted to go. He knew that seeing her would remind Yano of better times and he would begin to cheer up. Angie has always been a caring friend to Yano and always looks out for him. Yano knew this and was always appreciative as he was aware that working on controlling his temper was a rather large problem that needed fixing.

Arabella snuck out of her window and the three sat in the backyard and talked. They told stories of the old country, tales of their voyages across the ocean. They laughed, they connected, and for a moment in time, they lived like kids. There were no homicidal emotions brewing in Yano, there were no tears, there was no fear. Only talking and laughing like a couple of careless kids who still had their entire lives in front of them.

The Secret

AS YANO IS walking home, he passes Dino's place of business. Dino has seen Yano still running the streets with the gang and ignoring their previous encounter, and he has been wanting to speak with him again about it. Now here he comes, right in front of Dino. Dino steps out through the door and hollers to Yano.

"Hey, kid! Come here I want to talk to ya!"

"Not now!"

"Then when? You'll just ignore me again next time too. Come here it'll only take a minute."

"Not now!" Yano yelled.

"Hey! I'm not your little brother! I ain't one of these little punks you run with, you are NOT going to speak to me that way!"

Yano gives in and walks across the road to speak with Dino.

"Why do you spit in my face? Do I disrespect you?"

"I don't even know what you're talking about Dino."

"Oh of course you do. I told you about running with these little punks in the neighborhood. They're nothing but a bunch of thugs and will never amount to anything. They will never earn the respect of anyone else in their life. This is who you want to be like? I am not trying to bring up old news or say anything that'll upset you Yano, but your father, God rest his soul, your father would be disappointed."

With a clenched fist, Yano leaped at Dino. Another man from behind grabbed Yano and pulled him back before he could get at Dino. Dino is quite surprised by the amount of anger that Yano still shows. It has been almost three years since Enzo's passing and Yano, a nineteen-year-old boy, still has so much anger bottled up.

"Do you want to be a thug, or do you want to be a somebody?" Dino asked. "Because anyone who needs an attitude adjustment can be a thug, but it takes a real man, a man's man to be a somebody."

"I am somebody! Ask anyone around here, they'll tell you!"

"All that anyone around here will say is that you're a little punk who takes what doesn't belong to you! No respect! None gave, and none earned!"

"C' mon Dino, everyone knows me. Everyone respects me."

Dino laughs at Yano's outlook.

"People know you, yes, but people do not respect you Yano, and it's only people here, in our neighborhood that know you. What about the next neighborhood to the north? Or the South? There are other people in this city and none of them know you. So in the bigger picture, no, nobody knows you. You're nothing, but, if you're willing, I can help remedy that."

"Oh, you can make me known?"

"I can."

"City-wide?"

"Shit boy, I can have everyone in the next state fear your name, maybe even the entire country. That's all on you. You will only get out of it what you put into it."

Yano thinks that Dino is just talking to hear himself talk now. How could this old guy do anything of the sort?

"How can you help me, old man?"

"Better watch your tongue kid, this is your last warning! Showing respect to people goes a long way in life. Take that as your first lesson."

Yano nods his head as if to apologize to Dino.

"I am involved in what I would call, grown folks business. I do not make as much money as I would like because we have to keep our every move quiet."

"Because of the cops?" Yano asked.

"Na. We ain't worried about no cops. It's the Black Hand. They would take my entire operation from me if they knew."

Dino began to let Yano in on what it is he does for a living. It turns out that Dino is into criminal activities as well. His do not seem as dangerous though. Dino has been operating a small-time casino in the basement of his grocery store. He had a craps table and a few poker tables. In no way was he ever going to get rich off of his operation, though he did make a lot of money. If the Black Hand were not around he would be able to expand. Police can be bought, the Black Hand cannot. They would come to take the operation over completely and Dino would get in trouble for hiding all of this income from them.

Dino offered Yano a job as a bartender at the games. He told Yano that the pay was very good.

"Gamblers tend to lose, and losers tend to drink," Dino explained.

Yano listened as he was told how he could bring home almost triple every week than what he is making as a burglar. Yano just cannot see himself as a working man, taking orders from other people. It's just easier to take what he needed as he needed it. Yano turned Dino's offer down. He tried to explain that he thinks that the working man is a sucker. He can never take orders from another man, that's just not the way he is wired. All Yano could think is that he is his own boss, he makes his money how he wants, not the way any other man dictates.

No man has the right to tell another man how to make his way in life. These are choices that only we can make. We can be guided toward the right path, but *choosing* the path is on each individual.

Dino keeps persisting that Yano takes the job and get off of the street. He even tells him that the Black Hand has caught on to the Two Kingdom Boys' schemes and they are going to be taxed as everyone else has been. Yano shrugs it off and exits the store. As the door swings shut, Dino yells something. He yelled something that caught Yano's attention. Something that made Yano stop dead in his tracks. As Yano turned back around to look at him, Dino opens the door and repeated himself.

"I know who killed your father."

Yano is in shock. He has known Dino for a few years now.

"Why haven't you told me this before."

"I wanted to wait until you were old enough."

"Old enough for what? To kill a man? I could've pulled the trigger on that man the day after it happened! Why did you not tell me then?"

Dino understood how Yano was feeling, but he had to try to calm Yano down and explain to him that he was too young for vengeance at the time. He was only sixteen, and yes, he was old enough to pull a trigger, but he was not old enough for what else will come with it. Dino tried to explain that killing a man is not as easy as it seems. Pulling a trigger can be hard, and if you pull a gun on a man and are not fully prepared to go through with it, then it could go very badly for you. The act of killing a man does not stop after the bullet enters the flesh. It does not stop as the man falls, nor after the man's heart stops. The act of taking a life continues long after. The dreams that haunt you for years after, the guilt, the constant paranoia of being caught. No, the act of killing a man is no easy feat. It takes more than just a young teenager with tears in his eyes and a heart full of hate. It takes a strong body, mind, and soul t be able to live with the fact that a man is no longer here with his children and that that is your fault.

Yano looks Dino in the eyes and asks,

"It was the Black Hand, wasn't it? That killed my father. I have always had a feeling that they were behind it for some reason."

Dino explains to Yano that he still doesn't think that he is old enough for this. He only told him what he knew to get him to be smart. So that he doesn't get himself killed running with this stupid gang before he does get old enough.

"Let me give you this job, Yano, and when you truly are old enough, then I will help you with this."

"Hell no! I want to know now Dino! Who the fuck killed my father?"

Yano had tears running down his cheeks now as he insisted that he be told. Dino tried to do a good thing by taking him under his wing, but this is not going to end well. Yano is heartbroken all over again and in a worse way than he has been in years. Vengeance has to be handed down and Dino knew it as well as anyone else. Dino put his hand on Yano's shoulder and led him back inside the store. They sat and talked for a few hours. Dino explained everything that he saw that night. He then had to defend himself against Yano's backlash against him for not going out to help his father. Dino explained how there are not enough people in the neighborhood who are willing to go to war with the Black Hand, and that if he went out to help, he would've been killed as well. Who then would have told you what had happened? Who then would have spent the last three years looking out for the boys? Dino tried to explain to the best that he could that what he did, not rushing out to help Enzo, was what was best for everyone.

This organization is secretive. Gianni Spilotti is the only known enforcer. He is the face of the Black Hand. Other men are suspected, but nobody knows who else is involved. Everyone also knows that Gianni is not the boss of this criminal organization. Though he is big and dangerous, he does not have the brains to run an operation on this scale. Dino tells him that it was not Gianni who killed his father, it was another man from the neighborhood. He does not know his name and the only way to find out is through Gianni. Gianni may not be that smart when it came to books, but with street smarts, he is a regular Albert Einstein. He knows that if all possible, you distance yourself from a murder. So this man that killed Enzo was most likely a hired gun.

Name and ranks of Black Hand members are never spoken to outsiders, so to get a man like Gianni to talk is going to take brute strength and nothing else. Dino agreed to help Yano plan this out thoroughly as long as he agreed to walk away from the gang. Yano graciously agreed. The probability of Yano agreeing to about anything to get his vengeance was very high. The two sat down and tried to plan out the easiest way to get to him and how to take him down. Every time one of them thought of what they saw as the perfect plan, the other would pick it apart and find every hole. Yano finally told Dino that he wanted to bring in Angelo. Angelo was Yano's most trusted friend, and he was sure that he would walk away from the gang with Yano. Dino had his doubts, with never having met the kid before, however, if it got Yano to walk away from the gang he was fine with it.

When Angelo was told about the plan, he was skeptical. He wasn't sure that there would be a way for them to bring down Gianni. Angelo came up with many things that would go wrong, but in all actuality, he was just afraid. No one blamed him for being afraid either, for one reason, Gianni is a dangerous man, and messing with the organization is a death sentence if caught. The second reason he was afraid, it was the first murder any of them have ever thought about while having plans of actually following through with.

Angelo was finally convinced and had his nerves settle. Doing this is possible, hard, but possible. Angelo instructed Yano to spend a few days with Arabella.

"Stay away from Gianni!" He demanded.

"I will think of something."

Angelo followed Gianni for three days. Night and day, wherever he went, Angelo was behind him. In the three days, he didn't show any unusual patterns that could be exploited. He didn't even go home every night so getting him there would be hard as well. This plan was beginning to seem like it would have to be something spontaneous. If he doesn't have a routine then the boys would have to just follow him all night until he finally ended up someplace secluded. These sorts of plans do not usually work out so well. Angelo underestimated Yano's desire for this. He forgot that this had no meaning to himself but to Yano and Gino, it meant everything. Yano was willing to get him however he could.

Yano decided that he was going to surprise Gianni at home, even if he had to wait there for days. This is where he lives, this is where he is going to feel safe and comfortable to let his guard down, so this is where I need to hit him Yano thought. Angelo told him that Gianni keeps his spare key on top of the doorframe on the porch. The last time I watched him at home, he sat in his living room chair with a glass of wine and read his paper. Then he went straight to bed.

"Poison the wine?" the Gino suggested.

It seemed easy enough, sneak in, contaminate the wine, and then sneak back out again. All of this could be done before he ever got home. They could watch him from afar, through a window maybe. This seemed like a good plan to the others but Yano wasn't sure.

As Yano was preparing to act, he told Angelo and Gino both to stay home. They were upset but Yano was older than Gino and this matter didn't concern Angelo, so they both backed off. Dino walked Yano to Gianni's house and tried to explain what to expect. He again explained what killing a man does to you. You are never the same after committing such a heinous act of violence, no matter the reason. Yano understood but it was something that he had to do and Dino could do nothing but accept and respect his decision.

As the two approached the house, they noticed that the lights were on. They hid behind some trees across the street and peered into the large picture window. Gianni was already inside. He was already sitting in his chair, already had his wine, and his paper.

"How the hell am I going to poison the wine now? Shit, how the hell am I even going to get in now? Why is he home so early?"

"Don't worry about it, I'll think of something. You *are* going in there tonight, and he *is* dying tonight. That is all that I am sure of right now kid. Just head to the back door and wait."

"How will I know when to go in?"

"Oh, you'll know," Dino responded.

The Act

"**C**' MON DAD! Try and catch me!" Yano runs through the yard and around the tree as Enzo is chasing him through the yard. Yano is so happy, laughing, and running as fast as he can, trying to get away from his dad. Yano sprinted toward Gino who is playing on the tree swing, Enzo grabbed him and spun around with him a few times. They both grew very dizzy from the spinning and they tumbled to the ground laughing. Enzo rolls over and grabs Yano in a big hug and starts to roll around tickling him.

"Stop all of the horseplay and come eat" Fina yelled out.

Enzo stood up and grabbed Yano by the hand. They walked over and grabbed Gino. Enzo, holding Yano by the hand, carrying Gino on the other arm, walked towards their Sicilian home to eat lunch.

POP! POP! POP! The sounds of gunfire erupt and awoke Yano from his daydreaming trance. This must be Dino's distraction that he told me about. Yano quickly enters Gianni's home through the back door. This door led him into the kitchen. Yano peeked around the corner and saw Gianni on the front porch still yelling at Dino. Yano quickly jumped from the kitchen into the living room and hid behind the chair, fumbling around, trying to get the small bottle of poison from his pocket.

"Stupido Vecchio! (Stupid old man)" Gianni yelled.

He slams his door shut and drops his pistol on the end table. As he mumbles more in Italian, he approached his chair and sat. As Yano sat behind him, lurching in the shadows, he stares blankly at the bottle of poison. He did not get it in the wine, but it wasn't from a lack of trying. He knew that poisoning him would be too easy. Just the thought of knowing that he died at Yano's hands was not enough satisfaction. Yano wanted to feel the life drain from his body. Yano was beginning to feel so much anger that he forgot certain things, important things. The initial plan was not simply to come poison this man and watch him die, but to extract information. Information that is highly important in serving out justice to all involved. This would only have a small chance if Gianni was already poisoned, now... there is virtually no way Yano will make this behemoth of a man talk. Kill him or leave. These were the only options now.

As Gianni read his paper, he drank a few more glasses of wine. The incident in which Dino caused had him so worked up that he began to drink faster than usual. Yano waited, as he waited he slowly and quietly stripped the laces from his shoes. He held them both end to end, with one end wrapped around each hand. Yano took a few deep breaths and as Gianni took another sip, his last sip, of the Merlot Yano leaped from the darkness and wrapped the laces around this drunk man's throat. Gianni, half asleep and all surprised, gasped for air as he dropped his paper. Yano screamed for him to say one name.

"Just one name! I only want one name! Who killed my father? Enzo Scarpacci! Who did it?"

Gianni managed to mumble a few words,

"You will die in the streets... as your father did."

He tried to stand and as he did Yano's grip became loose. Yano's feet started to lift from the floor as this giant killer rose from his chair.

Yano was able to wrap his legs around the guy's waist and regain his grip squeezing even tighter than before.

Gianni spun his body around and as he did, he slammed his shin into the coffee table. This dropped him to one knee. Yano dropped one foot on the floor and dug his other knee into the man's back. As Yano's knee pushed on the man's spine, his stomach and chest pushed forward. Yano then pulled backward on the laces while simultaneously squeezing harder. The blood vessels began to pop in his face, eyeballs turned red, and his tongue seemed almost to swell from the pressure as it could no longer fit in his mouth. Within a few more minutes of squeezing, just before the laces would ultimately break, the body goes limp. The pressure on the laces is released as Yano feels that there is no more fight left, and the lifeless body slumps over the coffee table in front of them.

Yano had officially just taken the life of a Black Hand member. These guys are supposed to be untouchable. There will be havoc in the streets when other members learn of his death. No names were learned, no justice had been delivered, a man lay dead on his living room floor, and that is the only thing that happened tonight. There is no turning back now, killing every one of the members or being killed while trying is the only way to end this now.

The next day Gianni's body was found. Angry men with guns flooded the streets looking for answers. Yano was nervous, even swift minded Angelo didn't expect this. They both knew that there were sure to be some new faces in the neighborhood with some inquiries into the act, however, for the organization to roll in this deep and this armed was not what any of them expected.

Eleven new faces were spotted in the neighborhood that day, all hanging around Gianni's house. These faces were not unlike that of Gianni, though Yano didn't appear quite as afraid of these ones.

"I guess we need to figure out which one to approach and speak with first," Dino uttered.

"Speak? Why not just kill them all? They're not going to quit coming until they're all dead anyway. We might as well get started," Angelo responded.

Gino snickers, he tries to be tough, but Yano can see that he is afraid. Yano nods his head at Angie and looks at Dino. Dino shakes his head back and forth slightly and then gives Yano the nod of approval. None of them are exactly sure how an old man, two nineteen-year-olds, and a sixteen-year-old kid are going to go to war with the Black Hand and expect to win, but they are all more than willing to try.

The next day, Yano and Angie were at Dino's, kind of hiding out and trying to think of what to do next. All the while, Gino is out being a kid. He almost seemed to forget about what had happened in previous days. As Gino was outside walking around, he ran into a little Irish kid, Patrick, that he knew from school. The two started talking and walking towards Dino's grocery store for a snack. As they were talking, Patrick was tossing rocks at a fence and watching them bounce off. One of the rocks that he threw just grazed the top of this wooden fence. An angry yell could be heard from the other side. As the two boys peeked over the fence, they saw a large man with a small line of blood running down his forehead. The man saw the boys and yelled in Italian,

"You stupid kids!"

The man was a Black Hand member who happened to be passing by on his way to speak with some townspeople about Gianni's death, was already angry but now he is pissed off. He walked quickly toward the boys, first shoving Gino to the ground, then slapping the Patrick. Patrick fell to the ground as Gino was jumping back up. Gino had a fire in his eyes, he had never felt so angry. He jumped and tried to attack the man but was instantly thrown back down. The man leaned over and grabbed both boys by their shirts. He then screamed and dropped to one knee. He turned to look behind him and there was one of the other Two Kingdom Boys, Antonio Marducci. He had been passing by on his bike and saw Gino in trouble. He rode up behind the man as he was bending over and grabbing the boys by their shirts, Anthony picked up his bike and swung it back down crashing it into the man's back.

This man is a gangster, he is a Black Hand member. He is supposed to be feared and respected, but here he is, getting attacked by three boys who haven't even finished puberty yet. He was not going to stand for this. Getting hit with the bike hurt, not only his back but his pride. He reached down to pull out a gun. He drew his weapon and pointed it at Antonio. Right as his arm was lifting the metallic shiny weapon in a child's direction, Patrick was back on his feet and viciously attacking the guy. He was landing punch after punch, his knuckles bouncing off of the guy's cheek, then his eye, then the nose. The man grabs Patrick by the throat and slams him to the ground with enough force to break the sidewalk.

The sidewalk did not break, but Patrick's back did. The spine snapped, making the same sound as sticks cracking under your boot. His body lay motionless, his head in a pool of blood that leaked from the fractured area of the skull that bounced off the corner of the pavement. Gino stood there. He stared at his friend, at Patrick. He was in a state of complete awe, scared, upset, shock. He couldn't believe what had just happened. Before he could come back to down to Earth, Antonio had already pulled a three-inch blade from his boot and stuck it into the man's throat. Blood squirting, some on the ground, some on Patrick, some landing on Gino, but none staying in the man's body. The man yanked the blade from his windpipe, blood squirting from the jagged slit in the flesh. The man held his hands as tight as he could over his throat. He seemed as if he were trying hard to squeeze the cut back together. Gino turned to look at him, was he trying to keep his blood in, or was he trying to strangle himself? Gino couldn't tell, he just stands there and watches as the man bleeds all over the sidewalk. He watched as the man frantically gasped for one more breath of air, he watched this without the feeling of guilt, completely emotionless.

Antonio is yanking on Gino's shirt trying to get him to run away, but Gino just stares at the two dead bodies lying at his feet. He looks at the blood that had squirted on his shoes and his pants. Gino just kept thinking to himself, five minutes ago I was walking with my friend and laughing. Now He and another man are both dead. How did this happen?

Antonio was finally able to get Gino to leave the scene. Gino ran straight home, while Antonio went in a different direction. Antonio had just killed a Black Hand member in public, in broad daylight, and left his body lying in the street in a pool of blood. Antonio should have been murdered for what he did, he was fortunate that the police had found him before an angry group of Black Hand members did. Antonio was arrested and immediately taken to prison. Some people say he was lucky that the police got to him first, but these people do not understand how far the Black Hand's reach might go. Getting their revenge inside of prison would be just as easy for them as doing it outside of prison.

A loud crashing noise bursts through the air as Gino rushes through the front door of Dino's home, slamming the door against the wall. Yano, Angie, and Dino all jump from their seated positions. They had no idea what was happening or who was coming through the door. They were still on edge from the Gianni hit. Gino was stumbling all over his words as he tried to describe to Yano what exactly had happened. The sight of Patrick lying on the pavement twisted, in a pool of blood was too much for Gino to handle.

"He…He…He…"

"Calm down G! What happened?" asked Yano.

Yano held Gino by his shoulders, repeatedly telling him to calm down as he tried to put the words together. As Gino finally found a way to form a coherent sentence, his explanation for his breakdown was astonishing.

"Antonio, he did it!"

"Antonio did what?" Yelled Dino.

"He killed the man! He stuck his knife straight through the bastard's throat!"

Gino fell back on to the couch crying for Patrick. He was one of the first kids that Gino befriended when they arrived at the new neighborhood.

Later that night, Yano and Angie were sitting at Yano's house. They were sitting with Gino while he tried to recoup his state of mind after this tragedy. Yano, without saying a word, stood and walked to the kitchen and opened the closet. He reaches in and grabs the broom. Yano turned and looked at Angie. Angie just stared at him with curiosity, Yano says that he is going for a walk and instructs Angie to stay with Gino.

"Wait for a second Yano…" Angie started.

"Just do what I say, Ang. My mom doesn't need to know what's going on and you're the only one I trust to sit with him. I'll be right back"

Angelo nods and Yano walked out. Yano walks through the backyard looking around. He finally sees an old tree stump. He laid the broom handle on top of the stump, held it tight with one hand, and stomped hard on the long 10inch end piece that was hanging from the stump. It broke off with a long point. As Yano reached down for the broken piece, he through the other section to the side.

The Shadow Man

THE NEXT MORNING, Dino is awakened by screams from outside his bedroom window. Someone is angry. Something must have happened. Dino knew what Gino went through and he could not even begin to suspect what the boys had done. Somehow though, he did know that the boys had to have had something to do with it.

"You are going to die when we find you! You will lay bleeding in the street like the dog that you are!"

Dino sat up, shook his head, and stood up. He walked over to the window and peered down the street. Another body is lying in the alleyway. Another dead man. What are these kids thinking, Dino kept thinking to himself? He walks away from the window before anyone outside sees him starring and gets suspicious. That is the last thing that Dino needs is for the Black Hand to start looking into him. His entire operation would be in jeopardy. S Dino begins to dress for the day, he hears a noise. He reaches for the bedside table, opens the drawer, and pulls out his chrome six-shooter pistol.

Dino sneaks down the stairs only to find Yano sleeping in his kitchen, under the table. He notices the blood-covered clothes that Yano is wearing but sees no wounds. Dino shakes his head and kicks Yano slightly, just enough to wake him. Yano awakens, frightened. He sees Dino and quickly apologizes for breaking into his house.

"I didn't want to wake you, so I just slept on the floor."

"Under the table?"

"Yeah. The men were walking around, looking through windows. I didn't want them to see me."

Dino's kitchen table is pressed against the wall, under the window. Nobody peeking in could see anything except the other side of the kitchen.

"Did you have something to do with this…. this…. incident outside?"

Yano smiles smugly and shakes his head.

"There is nothing funny Yano! You have to stop this; you are out of control!"

"What are you talking about? Isn't this the path that you set me on? Revenge for my father, eliminate them to keep your card games safe?"

"There's more to it than that kid! You must be smart. You cannot just leave bodies lying in the street. That's not good for any of us!"

Dino stormed out of the room. He couldn't believe how stupid Yano was acting. He went back up to his room and collected some new, clean, clothes for the kid. As he walked back downstairs, Yano was sitting in the chair at the table.

"I noticed some of the Black Hand members walking around last night. I saw them from my window. I saw them, and I just lost it, Dino, after seeing Gino broken like that, I just lost it. I had to do something; I mean…He's my brother!"

Yano goes on to explain what happened after he snapped off the end of his mother's broom handle. He quietly crept down into the alleyway and hid in the shadows. The corrupted man walked past the shadowed man, and Yano leaped from the darkness. He lifted his arm and swung it back down as hard as he could. The man, who was a lot smaller than Gianni but just as dangerous, fell to the ground. He was knocked unconscious from the wooden broom handle. Yano grabbed the man by his shoulders and dragged him into the shadows.

As the man woke, Yano bombarded him with questions. The man had no clue who Yano was or what had happened. He only knew that some kid was kneeling on his throat with a sharp piece of wood digging into his ear. Though the man was a dangerous man, he was not as strong-willed as Gianni. He caved quickly to Yano's line of questioning with only a promise that his life would be spared. He explained that he does not know their boss, just that he is known as il Vecchio, the old man. He swore that he knew nothing about the murder of Enzo, and could say nothing as to who robbed him of life.

"It doesn't matter how many of us you kill. Even if you find out who shot your father, he is simply the messenger, and shooting the messenger has no meaning. If you are truly after retribution, then you need to find out who gave these orders."

Yano was told by the man that a guy named Salvatore Scarpone would be able to give him answers about il Vecchio. Answers that he was not able to give. As he said Salvatore's name, he was pleading for Yano to let him live. Yano lets the man sit up. He walked behind the man and bent down on one knee. He leaned forward and whispered into the man's ear.

"I let you see my face. I did this so that you would feel comfortable speaking with me. But I am done speaking with you, and I am afraid that I cannot let you live."

Yano reaches around and grabs the man by his forehead, spins him onto his side, and slams the sharp piece of wood into the side of his neck. The man screams, but only for a second. Hs throat quickly fills with his blood. The same blood that spits from his mouth as he tries to talk to Yano.

"Plea…Plea…Please…help…me."

The man drowns in his blood rather quickly, even quicker than Yano thought would happen. He glances over and sees an ax in the neighbor's yard. He had to send a message, a strong enough message to bring the boss's man Salvatore out of his hole. Yano jumps the fence and grabs the ax. He sees three more men walking towards the alley, though they are still about two hundred feet away. He had to make this quick. He swung the ax quickly but powerfully, and with one swipe, removed the man's leg at the knee. Another chop and the other leg was separated. Yano peaked around the corner again, the men were a lot closer now. Yano ran back and slammed the ax down again, chopping off an arm. He then took cover, back deep in the shadows. The three men walked by, not one of them even stole a glance down the alley. Yano left the darkness again and slammed the ax into the man's chest, lodging it into its final resting place.

This is a message and a violent one at that. It was saying that someone out here is not afraid of the organization and was standing up to them. This was going to upset a lot of the neighbors. They know that things are going to get worse before they get better, and they live right in the middle of it. For as long as Yano is an unknown assailant, then everyone in the neighborhood is a suspect. Other neighbors are given hope by these attacks. Hope that this vigilante was going to make a change. Everyone was on edge and everyone was walking on eggshells.

This kill was rushed, it was a mess, but it was serving its purpose. The organization was flabbergasted, they were completely and utterly stumped. They were also mad as hell and they began to look like headless chickens. They were all running around cursing the killer, but none of them knew which way to run nor which way to scream. Their actions became thoughtless and messy. They began beating men on site. If they couldn't find and punish the killer, then they were going to punish everyone. Men were being beaten in their shops, on the street, and in their own homes. The organization began raiding people's homes just to look for men to beat. In some instances, when a man was not around, the women were beaten.

It was only a week or two after the messy murder that Yano committed, and the talk began. The talk of a man, a very scary, dangerous man, was coming to town. People said that this was a man that people have only heard about, nobody sees him, and the ones that do, don't see anything for much longer. It was the devil himself coming to town, Salvatore, and it was rumored that he was coming for war. People spoke of the army that he was bringing. There was to be a massacre. A massacre of all men and young boys in the neighborhood. This would assure them that the killer was amongst the dead as they knew that a woman could never have pulled off these heinous crimes.

Dino scolded Yano and blamed him for any innocent deaths that were to come of his recklessness. Yano didn't argue with the fact, but he also did not want to hear it. He knew that any blood that was to be spilled would be on his hands. He did not want this, but he knew it cannot be avoided. When going to war, innocent people die and that is a fact that Yano stated time and time again. Dino had heard him say this a few times and was tired of it.

"These people are not soldiers, Yano! These people do not want war! There is no reason for any of them to die. The worst part is, they see what's happening around here as of late, though they know not why it is happening. They do not know why people lay bloodied in the alley, chopped to pieces. They just know that it is happening!"

Yano shrugged off everything Dino had to tell him. He understands what his point is, though cannot find a way past it. Gino is now sixteen years of age and still a kid, but he wants to help with whatever his brother has planned next. He wants to avenge, not only his father but also Patrick.

"What would be the best way to get to Salvatore?" Asked Dino. "How, exactly, are we supposed to touch the 'untouchable'?"

Angie and Yano begin to batt around a few ideas. Anything one of them said, another would show all the holes in the plan. None of them would work. Dino was also trying to think of ways, but to get face to face, unnoticed, to a man who is coming to kill all men and younger boys, would be almost impossible. He was not coming alone, and more than likely will always have at least five goons with him. He is a top man in the organization and these are not going to be the typical goons as Gianni was. These men are going to be the real deal, the most deadly of the organization. There has to be a way to get him.

As Angie was turning down another one of Yano's ideas, they heard Gino speak.

"From a hundred yards away!"

Everyone was confused as this made no sense to them. Gino just began blurting out words as if he were talking in his sleep. Yano looked over at him and asked what he was talking about.

"That's how we get him. From a distance, not up close. We don't have to figure out a way to get face to face with the man, because we don't *need* to get face to face with him. We can get him from a hundred yards away."

"OK," thought Yano, "But how Gino?"

"Explosives. Let's make a bomb and attach it to his car"

"How the fuck are we going to do that? That's ridiculous" exclaimed Angie.

"We don't know how to make bombs Gino, who the hell do you think we are?" Dino added.

"I do," said Gino. "Well, at least I think I do. Patrick used to talk about it all the time. His father used to make his fireworks. I think I can figure it out. We just need some wax paper, gunpowder."

As Gino was rattling off the bomb ingredients that he would need, Yano and Angie, look at him perplexed. They cannot believe what they are hearing, though neither of them shoots this idea down. They all know how dangerous this will be. Simply trying to make the bomb will be as dangerous as trying to use it. They know not what they are doing. The entire time, however, none of them say one thing about it being a stupid plan or that it will not work.

Dino opens the closet door and grabs a box of shotgun shells.

"Will this work?"

"Probably," said Gino, "Though we will need a lot more than this. The explosion has to be pretty big to kill him."

Dino finds a loose thread in this plan and begins to pull at it. The plan does seem to unravel a bit. At the very least, it needs more thought put into it.

"Well, how the hell are we even going to use it? We still must get close enough to speak with the man. Don't you remember why we needed to get to this man in the first place? We need to find out about the boss."

Blowing this man up would be pointless. More information is still needed, and he is their only lead to getting it. Another plan would have to be concocted.

The Diner

"DO YOU KNOW who killed my men?"

BANG!

"What about you? Do you know who killed them?"

BANG!

Scarpone was walking through the streets, asking people about the current events in the neighborhood. He was then shooting anyone who didn't have anything worth-while to tell him. In his eyes, he was making examples out of these men. Gino quietly followed him from a distance for days. He watched as innocent lives were struck from this world. Men woke this morning only thinking about the work that they had to do. They were all completely unaware that they had any chance of not coming home tonight.

Gino counted as the bodies of twenty-four innocent men fell on the floor bleeding over the last four days. He was appalled, and it bothered him severely that the others wanted to wait. The longer their actions were put on hold, the more bodies Gino had to watch fall limply to the afterlife. How were these people examples? Examples of what? Showing that anyone could be killed for any reason at any time? This didn't make any sense to Gino. The only example that should be made is to kill the killer. He then realized that Yano had been doing the same thing. He was killing bad men, who probably deserved to die. However, they did nothing to Yano, Gino, or even Enzo. Gino quickly reminded himself that the men were evil and that Yano was justified in his actions. Gino couldn't bring himself to realize that his big brother was slowly turning into what they were trying to stop. Gino wants to believe that what they are doing is different in some way, so that's what he forced himself to believe.

As Gino kept watch on Scarpone and learned his daily routine, Yano sat quietly in the back of the neighborhood church house. He sat there as the priest conducted the mass and thought of days past. He thought of his first holy communion and about the times that their family spent in church. He desperately wanted to receive communion like he always had before, but he now thinks that he is unworthy. The bible says an eye for an eye, and that is exactly what Yano is doing. Though he feels that he may have taken too many eyes compared to what was taken from him. The bible also states that you must turn the other cheek. This confuses Yano. How can you tell people to forgive and forget and then tell them to seek revenge at the same time? Would God understand and expect him to seek some sort of vengeance for his father? Or does he expect Yano to leave it be and move on? An eye for an eye, to man, is justification but still considered murder in the eyes of God. Yano felt unwanted in the church. As he looked around, he didn't notice anyone looking at him. There were no disappointed glances. This was because nobody else knew that it was, he who was killing these evil men and bringing death to the neighbors, but he felt as if it were the Lord who gave him the unwanted feeling. Yano knew that it was God's forgiveness that he was seeking. The entire time he sat in the church he asked God one question.

"Where were you when my father was killed? Where were you?"

His answer never came. He began to feel abandoned by the God that he once prayed to nightly. Yano stands and leaves the church and notices Gino standing across the street. He walks over and the two of them head back to Dino's. As they enter Dino's house, they hear him and Angie speaking.

"Look at how these assholes just come into our neighborhood and post up on the corners with the rifles! It pisses me off. What do you think is going to happen when their boss is killed? Do you think that the rest of the organization will just disband? That they will all just go their sperate ways?"

"Na," Angie replied. "The next in line will step up and replace him. A few changes will be made to start the new regime, people will be killed, and then it will be back to business as usual."

"But the new boss," Dino started, "Do you think that he is going to want to continue getting revenge for all that we have done?"

Angie shrugs his shoulders as if to say that he doesn't know. Yano interrupts, "So what if they do? We'll have to come for them before they come for us." Dino and Angie share a slightly uneasy look, neither of them is pleased with Yano's response. Yano asks the two if they have come up with any ideas. Neither have anything of any interest to say. Gino then says how he has been following Scarpone and knows where he is held up at. Yano says that the two brothers are going to go see Salvatore, and since there was still no plan, they would have to improvise. Dino tries to talk them out of it.

"Wait until we are there to help you. This is not going to be the same as the others. You will need our help."

Yano simply says that they cannot wait any more, and they were going to hit Salvatore Scarpone that night. The two brothers leave Dino's house and head down the street. They head towards the little diner that Salvatore has been eating his dinners every night since his arrival. The boys walk unnoticed passed the diner window, the squeaking noise of the door opening, also unheard. Salvatore Scarpone feels untouchable, what's going on behind him is of no concern to him. He is unaware of the two who would soon hold his fate in their hands sitting just a few tables away. The nervous, but brave brothers, watched as Scarpone unknowingly ate his last meal. He sat there eating a bowl of pasta and a big Italian sausage that was covered in peppers. He was completely unaware that these two boys are the ones he has been looking for, that they were the kids to whom his fate would be sealed.

As the boys sit and wait for their moment, like tiger cubs practicing their pouncing skills, a shadowy figure walks past the window. Scarpone looks up and smiles as if he knows the person. Just then the blurry figure approaches the front door and in walks Arabella. Yano quickly jumps from his seat and rushes over to her.

"What are you doing here?"

"Hey Yano, good to see you too."

"I'm sorry Arabella, it really is good to see you, but you really shouldn't be here right now."

"So, you're going to tell where I can and cannot eat now? Yano, I haven't heard from you in quite a while. I was afraid with all that has been going on in the neighborhood, that something may have happened to you."

"No, I'm fine. I can take care of myself. Please, Arabella, I need you to leave right now. I can't explain why; you just need to trust me!"

"Yano, you're scaring me. What's going on?"

"Please, Arabella, trust me. Just go to another diner, go home, go anywhere, but please do not stay here."

As the two spoke, Scarpone and his men begin to hear them and as they turn to see what is happening Yano grabs Arabella by the arm and leads her back out the door. Gino sits in his chair the entire time, nervous that Scarpone will see them and get wise to their suspicion. Luckily, they think nothing of it and as Yano and Arabella walk through the door, they go back to eating.

Yano convinces Arabella to eat somewhere else.

"I promise I will talk to you tomorrow. I will come to your house and explain everything."

"I hope so. I miss you, Yano."

"Ya, I miss you too. I have just been busy trying to right a few wrongs in my life."

Yano stands there in front of the diner and watches as Arabella walks away. As she turned the corner, she looked back at Yano for a second, and then continued her walk. Yano comes back in and sits down.

"That was close," Gino says. "They almost got suspicious."

"Ya, sorry about that. I couldn't let her be here when anything happened. I can't let her get hurt."

"Yano, it's fine. You don't have to explain anything to me. I care for her also; I saw how happy you were when you were with her. She's a good girl."

Scarpone's guards stood up and walked out of the building.

"This is it," Gino explained. "Every night, Scarpone finishes his meal as his guards go walk around the block to make sure everything is safe. His driver stays here though. Once he finishes his wine, he lights a cigar. Usually, right after this, the driver will get up and walk to the car."

"So, do we go now that the guards are gone and take out the driver also, or do we wait?"

"We should wait until the driver leaves. It will be easier to take down one man instead of two."

"What if the two guards come back in?" Yano asked as if he was getting cold feet.

"They won't, or they haven't at all that I have seen. They have always gone outside walking around the diner a few times."

"You're sure?"

"It's been the same thing every night, so I don't know why it would differ tonight."

Just then, Scarpone's empty wine glass touched back down in its final resting place on the table and his driver stood and began walking to the door. Yano tries to tell Gino to follow the driver out and stay outside to keep watch.

"You shouldn't be here for what comes next."

"Bull shit! They didn't just kill your father Yano; I need to be here too. I need to do this."

Yano nods at his little brother. He feels as if he needs to protect him from the nightmares that Yano knows so well caused by committing murder. He also understands Gino's need to be present when this happens. Just as Yano stands, one of the guards returns. The guard walks over and sits down at the table. Yano looks at Gino with a look as if telepathically asking if they have been figured out. Gino just stares back at his brother and whispers,

"We have to do this now. It may be our only chance."

Gino stands up and they both casually walk over towards Scarpone's table. Gino walks right past them as if he were going to the restroom. Yano walks right up to the table, grabs the bottle of wine, and smashes it over the head of Scarpone. The guard quickly tries to stand, but Gino moves faster. Grabbing a fork from a neighboring table, Gino grabs the guard from behind. With his arm around the man's forehead forcing his head backward, Gino jabs the fork into his eye socket with as much force as he could generate. The guard and Scarpone both fall on the floor, one un-conscience, the other screaming in agony as the piece of silverware protrudes from his face. The man tries to pull the fork out, but it doesn't come out alone. Part of the man's eyeball and enough blood to refill Scarpone's wine glass follows.

The site of this man's injury was enough to almost make Gino vomit. Instead, he picked up a butter knife. He sat down on the man's chest and pinned his arms under his legs. Gino waits for the man to let out another eardrum-shattering scream and then inserted the dull knife deep between the man's tonsils. There were no more screams at this point, just a gurgling noise as the man slowly drowned in his blood. It didn't take long, but Gino sat there, face to face, and watched the life drain from the man's body. He watched as all sign of life escaped those dark, killer eyes. Even though the bloody scene made him sick to his stomach, his actions were enjoyed. He felt an instant satisfaction knowing that his father was being avenged. He then let out a little smirk followed by a giggle as he remembered a line from the bible. An eye for an eye. He thought to himself how fitting this line was for this moment, only being brought out of his trance by his brother calling for him.

"Lock the door and help me get this fuck to the basement."

Gino runs over and locks the door and then shuts off the lights. The two drag Scarpone's heavy body to the back of the diner, down the hall, and down the basement stairs. There were spider webs in every corner, the air was damp. A smell was lingering as if Scarpone was not the only body that had been down here. Blood lay all over the floor, this must be where the butcher worked, cutting the diner's meat into slabs for steaks to feed the customers.

Once they get settled into the basement, the clock starts ticking. There is still a guard walking around outside as well as the driver out there waiting. One of them will surely return when they notice that something is wrong. They both run back upstairs and quickly begin to drag the guard downstairs. Gino picks up a butcher's knife, realizing that they would be able to dispose of the bodies easier if they were in smaller pieces, and without hesitation, starts cutting. Gino cut the man behind the knees, the elbows, wrists, ankles, and at the waist. As he stands there looking at the body parts, sort of admiring his work, Yano throws him a few garbage bags. Gino opens a bag, extends what is left of the man's arm, and slams the cold blade down again. Separating bone, skin, and tendons, the rest of the arm is removed at the shoulder. It seemed to remove all the pain from Gino's heart as he watched the blood squirt from the already stiffening corpse's wounds. No tears were shed for this man, nor for the actions that Gino chose to make. Just a kind of peace began to flow through him as felt relieved.

It took Gino less than seven minutes to dismember this man and get him into the trash bags. About the time that he was tying the final bag shut, Scarpone began to wake. Yano did not feel as prepared as Gino seemed to be. He was aware of what they were doing, and of the consequences, that would arise. Gino didn't seem to think about anything except finishing this part of their mission.

"We're going to need help. Go back upstairs and call Dino, tell him to bring firepower."

Gino ran to do what his brother had asked and left Yano alone in the basement with their next victim.

As Dino and Angie are heading towards the diner, they notice that Scarpone's man was walking in the same direction, he would be back soon. The two take a shortcut through the alley and end up in the back of the diner. They wait there until the guard gets close.

"You watch the driver, I'll get the guard," Dino tells Ang.

Angelo sneaked around the corner to the other side of the diner and gets closer to the car. Just as the guard unknowingly walks past Dino, Angelo jumps up and release a homemade firebomb at the car. A bottle filled with gasoline and oil shatters on the passenger door and the car explodes in flames. The dark, night sky is quickly illuminated by the orange and yellow lights. The driver is moving frantically as he escapes from the car. As he turns back, before he can even figure out what was happening, another flaming bottle is tossed his way. Shattering at his feet, the flames encased his body in seconds. He would scream and run around for just a few seconds before the fire burned through his nerves leaving him feeling nothing as he dropped to the floor. As the guard rushed over to see a puddle of melting flesh and charred bone, Dino was right behind him. He pulled out his pistol and let one shot ring through the still night air. The bullet spiraling from the barrel of the revolver and entering the back of the man's skull was the final noise. The two bodies were left on the street as Dino and Ang made their exit.

As all of this was happening, Gino watched the excitement from the diner's front window. He stared and watched as the man burned. He watched as the man's blood pooled from his head as Dino put a bullet in him. The morbid sights would be enough to screw with anybody's mind. It influenced Gino, but not with the effect that one would think. Gino began to change when he watched his friend get murdered, tonight's events made a definite change in him. He was nowhere near the innocent boy that he used to be. His mind liked what he saw. He quickly realized that killing is something that he liked to do. Something that he could quickly get good at. These thoughts made him feel dangerous.

As Gino made his way back to the basement, he saw that Yano had also made some choices that a normal person's mind could never fathom. Yano stood over Scarpone's body with a pair of hedge clippers. Scarpone's toes and fingers lay on the floor separate from his hands and feet. Yano dropped the bloody tool and picks up a hammer. Scarpone was yelling in pain but not talking. He would not tell the boys what they wanted to know. Yano lifts his arm and swings the hammer down hard, smashing Scarpone's ankle. The man still refused to name his boss.

"Who killed Vincenzo Scarpacci?" Gino yelled at him.

"Scarpacci? That's what this is all about? That bum?"

Scarpone snickers at the mention of the boys' father's name.

"You should be ashamed of that man instead of trying to avenge him!"

"Ashamed?" Yano asked.

"He was beaten and shot for no reason. He was put down in the street like a rabid dog! He had a family you son of a bitch!" Gino began to yell and lose his temper.

"Why would we be ashamed of a man who was nothing but a hard worker? A man who worked hard every day to provide for his family! A family who loved him!"

Scarpone's laugh could barely be heard through his painful cries.

"Hard worker? No reason? That man could not pay his debts. That is why he was killed!"

"Shut the fuck up and tell me! Who gave the order?"

"You know I cannot tell you that. You're an outsider."

Yano lifts his arm again and is ready to smash Scarpone's opposite ankle. Scarpone is a loyal man. He swore his life to an oath. An oath that is supposed to be unbreakable with the punishment of death. He has lived his entire life by this oath, this code of omerta, but the closer he gets to death, the less loyal he becomes.

"Are you going to deny a dying man his right to pray?"

"I don't intend on killing you. There are only two bullets left in my gun. One for the man who gave the order to kill my father, and one for the man who followed that order. I only killed your men to get your attention, you are making me take this further than I hoped it would go."

"What debts did my father owe?" Gino chimes in.

"Your father owed money to people. The type of people who you do not want to owe money to."

"What were the debts for?" asked Yano.

"He fell behind on his protection payments," before he could finish Gino interrupted.

"Protection from what? He was a stonemason he didn't need protection!"

"Everybody pays! One way or the other. If you fall behind on your payments to us, you die! If you fall behind on payments to the bank, they just take your house. Your father got a second loan on the house, so he didn't fall behind to us."

Scarpone started laughing, then finished.

"Then he fell behind on bank payments, so he borrowed from us. It didn't take long for him to fall behind again and, well, he got killed anyway. Now the only difference is that he left a bigger debt for your mother to pay back. He should've just died like a man years ago. This is the type of man you respect so much?"

Both boys cannot believe what they are hearing.

"You set him up to die. You knew he couldn't repay the loan."

"That's the way it works kid. Now, if you do not intend on killing me, then let me go."

Yano looks back at him with fire in his eyes. He now knows why his mother works harder than she needs to. She is responsible for the debts that were forced upon his father.

"I didn't intend on killing you, at first, but he more you talk the more you sealed your fate."

Scarpone looks back up at Yano with fear, "No, no, no, you cannot kill me!"

"Then give me a fucking name!"

"I can't," Scarpone cried.

"Then, you die."

"NO!"

Scarpone started as a true, soldato (or in English, a soldier), but every man has his breaking point.

"Sunny Paladino," Scarpone mumbles.

"Sunny is the man who killed your father."

"Who the hell is that?" asked Gino.

Scarpone continues, "He is a gun for hire. He has no boss, only contracts."

He goes on to tell the brothers that Paladino was staying at a farmhouse somewhere out of town. Though Vincenzo had been killed so long ago, the house belongs to Paladino's father so the chances of Paladino still being there were good. At least finding someone there who would know where to find him was a very high chance.

"And…" asked Yano.

Scarpone looked at the floor and shook his head as if to say, no, he was still not going to talk about the boss.

"AND!" Gino yelled.

Scarpone finally gives up and mumbles a name.

"Giovanni Talapini."

"That's your boss?" asked Gino.

Scarpone doesn't answer with words, just a few tears and a slight nod of his head. Talapini is a very cold-hearted man who was born in Palermo Sicily. He immigrated to the United States as a young man and became involved in ruthless events trying to establish a name for himself. He had spent four years in a Sicilian youth prison for burglary and another seven in the States for attempted murder. He was known as an all-around, bad guy.

Yano heard enough. The names are all that he needed, and he never truly intended on letting this man live. He swung his arm down one final time and let his hammer find a home inside of Scarpone's skull.

Yano looks over at his brother, "Bag him."

Gino turns and walks toward the shelf on the wall and grabs a few more trash bags as Yano grabs the cleaver and begins to prep the body for disposal. A few cuts here, a few more there, and the once tall, strong, body is in multiple pieces. This basement is used as a butcher's headquarters so the blood all over the floor should go unnoticed.

As the brothers carry all the trash bags, that are doubling as bloody body piece pouches, up to the stairs, and through the back door, Yano has an uneasy feeling. There are two dead bodies in the front, sirens can be heard in the distance. The police will soon be here. Maybe the lake of blood that he left in the basement will not go as unnoticed as he had originally thought. He then remembered the blood from the guard that Gino killed in the diner. It is a rather large pool smeared down the hall from where they dragged the body. That will definitely be seen.

Yano tells Gino to get out of here before the police show up, he has one more final task. Gino hid the bags in the bushes and took off. He ran as fast as he could, within minutes the sirens were very close. They must be at the diner by now. He turned around to see if Yano was anywhere behind him. All that he could see were giant flames. Flames appear to be coming from right where the diner stands. Or maybe, where the diner once stood, he thought.

Finding Talapini & Paladino

GIOVANNI TALAPINI IS one of the most violent men in America. He doesn't even try to live a double life, he is who he is and his family knows it. The entire neighborhood knows it. The man has been a criminal since birth. People say that his father was killed by police back in Sicily as he and Giovanni's mother tried to rob a bank. Giovanni's mother was apprehended while six months pregnant and gave birth to her son inside the prison walls.

Giovanni spends most of his days at home with his three daughters and his wife. He had two sons, but they were both killed trying to follow in their father's footsteps. He has a small room, his office, in the back of his house where he has meetings with his top guys. Out of respect, or maybe out of fear, they call him the Don. This word is derived from the old Italian word, dominus, which means master or lord. The word Don, which was first derived from Latin, came to mean a sign of respect for the boss of a criminal organization.

Getting close enough to clip Don Talapini was going to be the hardest thing that the boys have ever had to do. It is going to take a lot of extra planning than this Paladino hit, and since he is a hired gun, he may not even be in the neighborhood anymore. The rest of the guys were all able to convince Yano to find Paladino first. He may be harder to find if the farmhouse is empty but easier to hit once found, and besides, Talapini isn't going anywhere.

The two brothers meet up back at home after the diner incident. Gino sat there waiting for over an hour. Thoughts of his brother being caught, or worse, ran through his mind the entire time. As he left the room to get a snack, the front door swings open and in comes Yano. He slams the door behind him and quickly shuts off all the lights. Seconds after the house darkens, sirens from police cars come screaming down the street. They did not see Yano, though they saw someone running in his direction. It was too dark outside to make out any sort of description. This was a close call, but the necessary actions needed to be taken to hide the horrific scene at the diner.

Yano sat on the couch and snaps at Gino as he went toward the lights.

"Leave them off!"

"Yano, what the hell happened back there?"

"We left a mess. We were sloppy, let emotions cloud our minds and our judgment. We cannot leave evidence of any wrongdoing lying out in the open like that anymore. We need to be smarter. I heard the sirens coming after the gunshot. I knew that what we did would be discovered. I ran back down to the basement and grabbed a bunch of liquids used for cleaning and dowsed the place. I tossed a match as I fled through the back. The place went up in flames right as the police arrived."

"I saw the flames as I was running away, I thought something happened to you."

"I'm fine, but that was to close. We need to be smarter."

"What about the bodies? Were they found?"

"I don't think so. Where did you put them?"

"I stuffed the bags underneath those big bushes in the back."

"Well, we'll go back and check tomorrow. Hopefully, they're still there."

The brothers conversed all night about the events of the diner. They were both satisfied with what they did, maybe not how they did it exactly, but satisfied that is was done. They finally got some answers, answers that they have been searching for quite some time now. Or did they?

"I'm not too sure that I trust what Scarpone told us," says Gino.

"Why not?" Yano replied.

"He could've been saying shit just to try and get us to let him go. I mean, he thought he had a chance of living, so why would he tell us the truth? His boss would've found out it was him that ratted and then killed him anyway. I think it was all a lie."

"Well, it's all we have to go on. I don't think he was lying though."

The brothers went back and forth for a while until coming to the conclusion that what Scarpone had told them was unknown to be truthful or a lie. However, it was the only lead to finding Paladino that they had, so it is worth pursuing.

The following morning, the sun rose in a shade of pink and orange combination that can only be seen for a few quick minutes every morning. The birds were chirping, the breeze flowing through the windows blowing Fina's blue curtains back and forth ever so lightly. The boys both woke with one intention, finding Paladino. As they rose and headed to the kitchen for breakfast, a noise was heard. The neighbors outside were screaming. Yano went out front to see what was going on. People were crying in the streets. The news that the diner burned down was running through the ears of everyone awake. Yano couldn't believe that everyone was so disappointed about the diner. He looked down the street and saw Arabella, she was crying as well.

Yano walked down to speak with her but as soon as she saw him she turned to walk away.

"Arabella!"

As she slowed, Yano ran up and jumped in front of her. He held her by her arms and asked what was happening.

"Oh like you don't know."

"I don't. What's wrong?"

"Why did you rush me from the diner last night?"

"No reason, I was just having dinner with my brother."

"Oh. So because you want to have dinner with Gino, at a public place, I am not welcomed in the building?"

"No, no, no. That's not what it was. Arabella, I don't know if you noticed who else was there,"

Arabella quickly interrupted, "I don't give a shit who else was there Yano! Don't lie to me! I know you had something to do with it!"

"With what?" Yano tried to act as if he had no idea what she was speaking of.

"Maria, the owner of the diner, she was killed last night."

Yano was blown back a step. He went from pretending to not knowing what she was talking about.

"What do you mean murder? You think I would kill an old woman?"

"She was in the diner when it burnt. Hiding in the closet with two other bodies. They were burned so bad that the police have no id on them."

It cant be. Yano doesn't remember seeing anyone else in the building. He distinctly remembered looking all around before he and Gino made their move. Where could she have possibly been? And two others? Who could they have been? Waitresses? Cooks? Yano could not believe what he was hearing, Maria was the nicest woman in the neighborhood. When their father was murdered, she brought food over every night for two weeks so that Fina could mourn in peace. Her daughter, also named Maria, would also come over and help out around the house.

"Was it her daughter in the closet with her?"

"Noone knows Yano. I think its quite suspicious though how you told me to go somewhere else. You said that you would explain it all tomorrow and then rushed me out. Then within the hour, the diner burns down? Well, it's tomorrow Yano, explain!"

"I don't know what to say, Arabella. I can't believe that you would think that I could do something like that to her. Don't you remember how she came to my house and helped after my father died? How could you even think that of me?"

Yano turns and walks away. As Arabella yells for him to stop and come back, he ignores her and continues back up the street and back into his house. Yano tells Gino that they have to leave. Gino is curious but Yano rushes him out without any explanation. They walk to Dino's place in complete silence. Gino has a million questions but he sees a slight watery effect happening in his brother's eyes, so he remains silent. Yano walks into Dino's shop, sees him busy in the back, and walks back out. Before he makes his exit he grabs the keys from the counter. Gino is worried about his brother but remains silent.

"Get in," the only words muttered by Yano the entire walk. The boys borrow Dino's car, without him knowing of course, and begin driving towards the Diner.

"Are you going to tell me what's up?"

"Not yet. First, we have some unfinished business."

The boys drive up to the pile of charred wood and crumbled stone that was once a popular neighborhood feasting spot. There were people everywhere, all talking about what had happened. Yano pulls around back, on the neighboring street. They had to cross through the lawn of an elderly couple to get to the bushes where the bloody bags were hidden. The brothers both ran through the lawn and dove under the bushes and tried to retrieve the bodies. Gino didn't shove the bags under the bushes to far so they were hard to reach from this side. The two had to lay on their bellies and crawl under. The pokey branches and thorns snagged their shirts and tore at their skin. Finally, the bags were all collected, the boys each grabbed handfuls of plastic and sprinted back across the lawn.

As the two brothers were running, the elderly woman is watching from her window. She knows not of what they do, though she does notice something odd. One of the bags has a hole in it, perhaps torn open by a thorn in the bushes? Leaving a trail down the back of Gino's white t-shirt, a red liquid poured a steady stream from the ripped section. She is old, but not blind. She says nothing of what she sees, but she does know that the brothers are up to something unusual. She watched as they tossed the bags into Dino's trunk and fled the scene almost completely unnoticed.

"Where are we going, Yano?"

"Where the hell do you think? We have to get rid of the bodies."

"No shit, but where?"

"Well, we have to drive out to the farm to look for Paladino, so I figured we'll just get rid of them out there somewhere."

"Where?"

I don't fuckin' know Gino! I have never been out there before! We'll find a spot, relax already will ya?"

Gino sat back in his seat, turned his head towards the window, and sighed.

"Well, will you at least tell me what was going on in the neighborhood this morning? What were all the neighbors talking about?"

"It was about the diner."

"Really? The entire neighborhood was that distraught over the diner?"

"Yep."

Yano doesn't know how to tell his brother that he is responsible for the death of Maria, as well as two others. He tries to lie so Gino doesn't get himself too worked up with grief, he doesn't want his brother to back out of their plans. Though he tries, it doesn't work. Yano has to talk about it with someone and who else could he trust other than the person who helped him murder people?

"Maria is dead."

"Maria? The one that helped mom out after dad died or her daughter?"

"The mom… or maybe both. I don't know. The mom is dead for sure though."

"What are you talking about? How the hell did that happen?"

"She was there, that night."

"She was where? What night?"

"At the diner, last night."

Gino stares at Yano as he tries to figure out what he is saying. He remembers everyone leaving before they made their attack. The place was still open for business though, so someone *had* to have been there. Gino realizes that he only looked for customers as witnesses and didn't even think to check if the workers were still there.

"Where was she? Did you kill her?"

"Apparently I did."

"How? Why?"

"She was hiding in the closet with two other people, they must have seen what we were doing and got scared. I didn't know that they were there. They died in the fire."

"She was an innocent, Yano."

"I know."

After a few minutes of silence between the two Gino looks back at his brother.

"Well, maybe this is a good thing."

Yano looks at his brother with disgust,

"What the hell do you mean by that?"

"Well, they were witnesses, right? We would most likely be in jail right now if they had lived and told on us."

Yano shakes his head, half in disbelief that his little brother thinks this way, and a half in disbelief that he, himself, didn't think of it this way. She was innocent and didn't deserve to die. The other two corpses were probably the same. Though, Gino was right. They *were* witnesses, and no matter how hard, if they want to complete their objectives, any and all witnesses must be left to the afterlife.

The Farm

FOR JUST A little over two hours, the brothers drove. Down a long, dusty, one-lane, gravel road. The farmhouse that Paladino's parents owned seemed to never come. The hope that it was just over the next hill flooded each brother every time another hill hid the horizon. Gravel flying from their tires, dust filling the car. It was getting dark, and a little hard to see, but finally, on the other side of one hill stood a large house. As the boys got closer, they noticed it was more than just a house. There was a barn in the backyard, a sty full of rather large hogs, and uncooped chickens running wild.

"This looks like a farmhouse to me," Yano said with a grin.

"I hope it's the right one," Gino replied.

"I don't care if it is or not right now, I have to take a piss."

Gino laughed as his brother jumped from the car and began urinating in this stranger's yard. He then realized that he also had to go. As the two stand indisposed in the yard, one on each side of the car, they were able to look around from almost all angles.

Gino felt as if he were stating the obvious but still spoke out loud,

"This place looks abandoned like nobody has been here in quite some time."

"I agree. It looks as if it might have been a bust driving all the way out here."

"I fuckin' hope not. I don't want to drive all the way back home already. I need to be out of that sardine can for a while."

The trip was long, too long to end up being a waste of time. Over two hours of driving for nothing? This cannot be. At the very least, they found an area in which to bury these bodies that are far outside of their neighborhood. This home has no neighbors for miles, probably no cops coming out this way too often either. The perfect place to make somebody disappear.

Yano and Gino begin to walk around the large yard and look for shovels.

"This is a fuckin' farm! How is there no shovels lying around?"

"Chill out Yano, we'll figure something out."

The two continued to walk the farm when suddenly, from down the long road, a noise. It sounds like a car, maybe a truck. Just then, the dust being kicked up from the tires could be seen through the glow of headlamps. There is only one road in and one road out of this property. This has to be a resident, but could it be Paladino? Not the mother or father, but their murderous son? Could he be completely ignorant of the fact that he is driving right towards his demise at this very moment? The faces of each brother widened simultaneously as their giant smiles pushed their cheeks back towards their ears. Could this be the beginning of what they have been working towards for s long now? The moment that they have both been yearning for since the day that their father was so violently struck down?

They both jump behind trees as the car pulls closer towards the house. He drives up the driveway, parks, and a figure steps out. It is too dark to tell, but the driver appears to be younger. It has to be him. The dark silhouette of the unknown person walks up to the front porch. As

Yano turns tries to lean closer for a better look, SNAP! A stick is broken under his boot. The man looks over but Yano is too far and is unseen. The man pulls out his pistol and begins to explore. He heads towards the tree that Yano is hiding behind and points the barrel of his revolver in his direction. As he slowly creeps around the tree, almost discovering Yano on the other side, a loud thump rings through the dusty night air. Gino was able to remain unheard as he crept around his tree, up behind the man, and hit him over the head with a fallen piece of branch.

Yano lets loose a sigh of relief as he witnesses the man's body fall to the ground. When the man comes too, he is still on the ground, in the grass. Yano and Gino both standing over him. He reaches over for his pistol, but it is no longer there. It is now in the hands of a son seeking vengeance. Gino lifts his arm, points the barrel now in the downed man's position,

"Who are you," he says.

The man looks up at Gino,

"Who am I? This is my property! Who the hell are you?"

"You own this place?" Yano asked.

The man turns his bloody face towards the other brother,

"Yes, sir I do. Well, my parents do."

That was enough for Yano, he didn't take into account that the man they are seeking may have siblings. Gino, however, does need a bit more assurance. He is not the type that will kill just anybody, they have to deserve it.

"What's your name?" he asked.

"Paladino… Sonny Paladino."

Gino looks over at his brother and smiles. It *is* him. Neither could believe it. They thought it would be easy but not this easy.

Sunny begins to plead with the brothers.

"Please, you got the wrong guy."

"How do you know? Do you know who we're looking for?" Gino asked.

"No."

"Then how the fuck do you know that you're not, in fact, the *right* guy?"

"Vincenzo Scarpacci," Yano utters.

Sunny says nothing. He doesn't even look up, just stares down at the grass he sits in.

"Sound familiar?"

"Doesn't ring a bell."

"Really? Do you beat that many men and then shoot them for no reason that the names are not remembered?"

Yano begins to get angrier as Sunny pretends to know nothing.

"Grab his arm, Gino."

The brothers pick up Sunny's body and walk him over toward a wooden fence and lean him over it.

"In school, a few years ago, I read that a hungry hog can devour a human body in just a few hours. There are multiple hogs in this pen, and they all look pretty damn hungry to me. I'm betting you don't last more than twenty minutes in there with them."

"What do you want from me? It was just a job! Just a job! I don't know why he was killed. I didn't decide to do it for my benefit, I was ordered to handle it! Lease! Don't hurt me, don't kill me!"

Yano leans in close and whispers into Paladino's ear,

"How many times did my father say that to you before you shot him?"

Sunny looks up at Yano, then looks over at Gino.

"Father?"

Gino, with a tear in his eye, answers back'

"Ya, he was our father, and you took him from us."

"No, no, no. please. I'm sorry, it wasn't personal. It was just business."

"Just business? Well, it was extremely personal for us," says Yano with a sort of crackling in his voice.

This is the moment that they have both been longing for, well, one of them. Now that the time has come, what needs to be done is even easier than they had imagined, though, it was harder to watch. Not because of what happens next is too violent for them, but because their vision is blurry. Blurred with tears. Tears of happiness. Tears of sadness. The vengeance of their father was satisfying, though his face was now in both of their minds, reminding them of the way he looked, the way he sounded, the times they had together. Would he approve of what they are doing? Maybe not, but if the tables were turned, and it was one of the brothers murdered, Enzo would probably be seeking vengeance of his own.

The brothers each grab Sunny by a leg and flip him over the fence. He quickly tries to get up but slips in the mud. He jumps up a second time, a successful time, and dashes back towards the fence. Yano pushes him away and he slips and falls again. As Sunny hops up a third time, Gino uses his pistol against him, shooting him in the kneecap. This knocked him down for the final time. It also startled the hogs. Four of them awoke and noticed something in their muddy home. Was it feeding time? They haven't been fed in a while, they almost seem confused. They looked so mistreated and food-deprived that the brothers were both surprised that they didn't eat each other. The hogs came slowly, snouts up, sniffing the air around Sunny.

The hogs get closer to Sunny and begin sniffing. It doesn't take long for one hog to take a bite, then a second hog decides to take a little taste. Before the brothers knew it, all of the hogs were biting and tearing flesh and smashing bone. The teeth of the hogs tear flesh from Paladino's body as easy as a pair of sharp scissors rips through a piece of paper. The screams coming from Sunny are loud, they are painful, deafening, they are of a desperate man instantly regretting every life decision he had ever made. The hogs were so hungry, they didn't stop eating even for a second. It is surprising to watch animals eat this fast and not choke. The hogs each had their spot but as Paladino moved around, the hogs did also. As the hogs moved, they bumped into each other and started to fight, and take bites out of each other. They were each trying to get as much of Paladino as they could. Yano stares at the gruesome scene, appendages are torn away, and organs hanging out at this point. Sunny, no longer conscience, possibly not even alive anymore, just stays in a limp position. As one hog sucks intestine up like a piece of spaghetti, Yano looks over at his brother.

"Go grab the bags, Gino."

Gino headed back to the car. He didn't even pop the trunk, he knew that there are too many bags to carry alone. He jumps in the car and backs it up to the pigpen. As he walks to the back, he opens the trunk and the two begin to toss the body parts into the pen. They have had time to start the decaying process, and the stench was rancid. It was similar to the spot in town where cows were taken to be slaughtered, the cow kill house is what they always called it. The smell of the organs, eyeballs, hooves, and other unused, unedible, parts were tossed into a dumpster out back, and in the summertime, the smell can be detected for miles. Waking up on a hot summer morning, breathing that first deep breath of summer air as you yawn, and filling your senses with the smell of rotten cow parts (wrapping them around your taste buds, one could almost taste the death) is enough to make anyone vomit right there in bed.

The hogs wasted no time, it was food. Sunny was pretty much devoured so all but one ran over towards the bags. The bags were shredded and the maggot-covered, body parts began to disappear. It was disgusting, though an incredible site for the boys to witness. Yano knew of this, though he had no idea that it happened so fast. When the brothers finally decided to leave, a couple of hogs went back and laid down and a few were still snacking on and searching for the few remaining pieces.

The two began their journey back home. Gino didn't want to drive in the dark, but Yano didn't want to stay unless Paladino's parents were to arrive home during the night. He would not be caught sleeping, so Gino climbs in the back and closes his eyes, and Yano begins the long drive home.

Now, with only Giovanni Talapini left to find, Yano begins to feel as if their mission is almost complete. With Gino half asleep in the back, he was left alone with his thoughts. He started the drive off trying to plan out a way to hit Don Talapini but ended with thoughts of worry and sorrow. What was he going to do once this was all over? When Talapini is gone, then what? Will he go back to school? No, he is at graduation age by this time, it is too late to go back to school. Gino though, Yano will make Gino go back to school, this is a must. They were not going to live this lifestyle forever. This is not what Enzo and Fina moved their family overseas for.

The future looks quite dim for Yano, he has no experience with anything, except killing. He could hook back up with the Two Kingdom Boys (if there were any left alive or not incarcerated by that time) but what would they do? Rob stores? Steal cars? This is not what Yano wants, he doesn't want to become a different Blackhand organization, though it's beginning to look as if that is all that is out there for him. Maybe he will get back together with Arabella if she'll have him back. She is the only girl that Yano has ever loved, and it kills him inside knowing that while all of this is happening, there is no way to be with her without putting her in danger. He wants her back, the way she made him laugh, made him feel, the way she loved him. This is what is missing in his life, though whether or not she feels the same still is a mystery to Yano.

Yano has had a taste, not a taste, but a huge bite of the dark side. How can one go back to a normal life, having fun, and beginning a family after they have had a bite such as this? Committing murder destroys a small piece of your soul, and Yano has done this a few times now. The murders he has committed were violent, brutal, events, and he has more planned yet. Does he have, or will he have any soul left when he is finished?

The drive home seemed even longer than the drive out to the farm. Yano had nothing but time to think. His mind filled with questions, questions that no matter how hard he thought, he could come up with no answers. In order to get his mind off of these thoughts, he tried to think of pleasant times of days passed. He thought of the boat ride over from Sicily. The way that the ship crashed into the waves. The way that he was so afraid that the tiny ship would sink. He thought about how much Gino and Rosaria cried with fear and the way that their father comforted them. Yano pretended as if he was not afraid, he tried to show his father that he was strong. Enzo would not have cared if Yano was also afraid, he would have shown him the same comfort as the others. Yano listened to the words that his father spoke to his younger siblings and, even while pretending that they didn't apply to him, he felt safer listening to his father's words.

He then began to think of Arabella. These were both happy thoughts as well as sad. Yano missed the days when he would wake up with her in his thoughts. The days that he would skip school and meet up with her somewhere that they could hang out without being seen. As his eyes began to swell with tears, missing his one love, he noticed that the neighborhood was coming into view. Their home was right around the corner.

As the boys pulled back into the neighborhood, they drove straight home to get a few hours of sleep. When they awoke that morning, they headed out to see Dino and Angie at Dino's store. After Dino finished yelling at Yano for stealing his car, he decided to tell them what had happened while the brothers were gone.

"Ang and I went scouting around last night. We saw some suspicious-looking fellas and tailed them back to a rather large house."

"Talapini's house?" Gino interrupted.

"Well," Dino started again, "We can't be one hundred percent sure, though the place was very heavily guarded, s I'm thinking that it is."

The brothers looked at each other with excitement.

"How are we going to do this?" Asked Yano

"Were there any weak spots? Any areas that weren't guarded?"

Angie nodded his head, "Ya. There is one side of the house, there are guards, but it is very dark. No lights, just a window. I say we burn the place down."

"How will that ensure that Talapini is killed though?" asked Gino.

"It won't, but the flames ill make him exit the house. I think we should scatter around the compound, each in the eyesight of a door, and just kill everyone who comes out. Talapini is bound to come out of one of the doors, he isn't going to stay inside and burn."

This plan seems quite primitive, something is bound to go wrong but they all agreed. It is much easier to make him leave the house and go in the direction of the assassins, rather than to sneak past all of the guards, climb inside a window, and kill him in the house.

Yano is excited for this to all be over,

"How will we burn the house down?"

"Firebombs," Ang said. "Just like at the diner. We would need to toss a few into a few different windows to make sure that the flames spread through the entire house. I think that that will be the hardest part."

"Ok," says Gino, "So we're going to need two of us running around with firebombs while two of us watch the exits?" This seems like a longshot. I mean, what if he comes out of a different exit than we expect? What if we're not near that one and he escapes?"

"No," Dino begins the way he thinks they should do it.

"One person is going to run around with the firebombs. As long as you get two or three inside, the place should go up quickly. "Two more guys guarding the two main exits, and one last guy in the driveway. This way if he des sip passed the exits we're watching, we'll catch him in the driveway. He won't get away, this will be our only shot at this, we have to be extremely smart."

The four sit at Dino's and talk and almost celebrate the fact that their mission was coming to an end. They all had a few drinks, told some jokes, and laughed. This was the first time that they all hung out with each other and just had fun. The first time that they didn't have murderous thoughts clouding their minds, bad attitudes against each other, a truly happy day that each of them, especially the bothers, desperately needed.

Brothers in Arms

THE NIGHT WAS cold with heavy winds and rain. All four conspirators sit waiting, impatiently, for the rain to settle down. It seems as if a monsoon was coming. If the rain doesn't let up soon, a flood is sure to happen. The assassins all sit under a tree, but staying dry is a harder task than their actual plan for tonight. As they sit there, Gino looks at his brother.

"What are you going to do when this is all over?"

"If we end this tonight, then I have no idea what tomorrow will bring. One thing is for sure, you're going back to school."

"Oh, I know."

Gino had thought about the day that he returned to school on a few occasions. Not so much for the education, but rather, just to get back to being a kid. He missed hanging out with his friends, though it has been so long since he could live life without looking over his shoulder constantly, he wasn't sure if he would be able to go back to just being a kid. Yano is still confused and troubled by this thought. Going back to school is not an option for him, he'll never make it through college, and going back to the neighborhood street gang just seemed immature to him now.

"One thing I do know, whatever I do, I want Arabella to be there with me."

All three glanced at Yano, and then back at each other. They all feel as if the relationship that Yano and Arabella once had can never be rekindled. Yano is a different person now, and Arabella has an idea of what he has been up to. Yano is a killer, he hates what these people have made him become, but at the same time, he enjoys it. He is good at it.

After a few hours of waiting, the guys are rewarded. The rain doesn't stop but it slows down tremendously. The giant raindrops that were once falling like a faucet running over them is now a slow trickle of small, light rain. The four dedicated assassins make sure that their pistols or loaded and pockets are full of extra bullets. Angelo grabs a couple of his homemade firebombs and, as Dino sits discretely in the shadows of the driveway, the three creep towards the house. When they get close to the house, they notice that nobody is outside. The rain must have forced all of the guards inside, what started as a bad omen made their murderous plans seem easier.

Angelo handed each of the brothers of firebomb and a book of matches.

"Count to sixty, then let's burn this bitch to the ground. One... Two..."

As Angelo began counting, he and Gino ran to different sides of the house. Yano sat where he was and continued to count. Once he reached sixty he struck his match. Nothing. The book must have gotten wet. He struck another, then another, still nothing. As he was about to try another match, there was a crash of broken glass and then the darkness turned bright with orange lights. Gino must have gotten his to work. Suddenly another flash of light, Angelo's also worked. The house began to burn and gunshots started going off as the boys were shooting escapees.

Yano tried once again, and to his amazement, the match head sparks and creates a small flame. Yano lights the firebomb and throws it toward the open window. The bottle is wet, as is his hand. The bomb slips from his hand and misses the window. It crashes on the side of the house next to a door, and just as the flames burst, the door opens. Three guards try to exit but the flames quickly spread and consume them. Yano jumps from his hiding spot and rushes over towards the door with both guns out, firing bullets into each of the burning bodies.

The bomb that Gino threw into the house, exploded in a room where four guards sat playing cards, burning and killing them almost immediately. Angie's bomb went through a bathroom window which, at the moment, had no occupant. The flames still spread throughout the bathroom and down the hall where it joined Gino's flames and created one massive fire on the top floor. Yano's bomb began to burn upwards from the outside, climbing the wall and reaching the roof in seconds. The first part of the plan was working almost flawlessly, the house was ablaze. Now to wait for Talapini to exit and kill everyone else who escaped the flames.

Two more men coming running outside, guns are drawn, but before they could even see anyone, Gino fires. The bullets entering the men's heads and exiting with a large blood spatter pattern all over the side of the house. As the two bodies fall, Gino quickly begins to reload. More shots ring out and startle Gino, he drops his bullets in the grass. As he drops down to recover them, a bullet whizzes past his head. He looks up and sees a man running right towards him. Just as fast as he was running forward, he was blown backward when the loud blast of Dino's shotgun erupts. Gino looks back and thanked him. As Dino helps him up, a rumbling came from the house. The two look up just in time to watch the staircase collapse under the flames. Nobody else would be escaping through this door. The two split up, Dino runs towards Yano, and Gino runs towards Ang. Gunpowder exploding on both sides of the house for what seemed like an eternity, the men, the guards that Talapini had seemed to never stop coming.

Eventually, the guards stopped coming, the gunshots stopped filling the silent night air, and the bodies stopped falling. The entire house was now on fire, anyone else left inside would not survive. All four boys meet up around the front and watch as the house burns. The rain seemed to stop completely as if God wanted this to happen. Firetrucks were not coming, the rain was no longer pouring, this fire was going to burn all night. The four stand in the warming glow sharing smiles. Their job is over, it is done. Before they know it, their joys would be as shattered as the windows that they threw bombs through just minutes before. From somewhere in the darkness behind them three more gunshots ring out through the fire crackled air. All three bullets finding a home in Yano's back.

Before any of the boys see Yano's body fall, they all turn and return fire. After the first shots are let loose, they realize that they are shooting at cops, but it's too late to stop now. A gunfight between the good guys and bad guys begin. The night illuminated by the flashes from the pistol barrels, Dino's shotgun firing, Angie's pistols, the guns from all of the cops, looked like a ground-level firework show on the fourth of July. Gino is pointing his gun behind him and shooting as he runs to getaway. He stops behind a car and continues to shoot as Ang and Dino make their getaway. It was almost military precision the way they made their escape. One running a few feet and laying down cover fire, the next two running even further so Gino can get further away.

When Gino finally realizes that Yano isn't with them, its impossible to get back to him. They have run so far away and the cops have advanced their position passed Yano's almost lifeless body. Dino grabs Gino by the arm and drags him to the car as Gino fights and screams for his brother. The three make it to the car and get away unscathed. After the shootout, Yano's body lay helpless in the wet grass along with the bodies of six dead cops, and three more wounded.

The word of what happened spread through the neighborhood rather quickly. Everyone knew that Yano was shot and was in the hospital. They all knew that he was responsible for the fire, and the lives of the dead and wounded cops. They all knew that he was responsible for the massacre of Talapini's men. They all also knew that he had accomplices who had gotten away, everyone looked at Gino with suspecting eyes. Everyone knew that he was there, though the identity of Angie and Dino was still unknown. The neighborhood hated the violence that had erupted in recent years. It was a well-known fact that the Blackhand was responsible for most of it, and the rest that was still unknown for sure, the Blackhand must have had something to do with it.

Everyone knew the Scarpacci family, and no one expected that the brothers could be capable of this. After the news came out about Yano being responsible, the neighborhood remembered what had happened to Enzo, and it all started making sense. People hated the Blackhand, so hatred towards the brothers for their part was small, but the lives of the innocent that were lost were too hard not to blame them. Their need for vengeance, and their need to make the neighborhood safer, ultimately made it worse, more dangerous. Their thoughts of retaliation were understood by all, but their actions hated by most.

The Aftermath

THE FIRE AT Talapini's home burned almost all night. Once the flames had finally died down, and the charred wood cooled enough, investigators were allowed to enter. Bodies dead from gunshots lay all over the yard, some with burns from the fire. The bodies of eight more people were located inside the rubble, burnt to badly to be identified, Talapini could have easily been one of these bodies, but he was nowhere to be seen outside. Considering him to be dead is what authorities did, though no one knows for sure.

Even though Don Talapini's death is still uncertain at the moment, the neighborhood seems to have changed. The people walk the streets again as if this were the first day in years that the sun has shone through dark storm clouds. People were more cheerful, they seemed to enjoy their days more, they seemed as if they felt safe again. Gino and Fina both know that Yano has to go away to a scary, undesirable place for quite some time because what he did was horrible. At the same time, what he was responsible for was creating something beautiful. Though horrible as it were, sometimes ugly situations are needed to restore the power of beauty, and Gino feels good thinking of it this way and knowing that he was part of it. Fina, on the other hand, hates what her son did. No matter what the outcome, and she looks at Gino with a look of disgust. She knows he was involved, as their mother, she could always see right through their lies.

The neighborhood truly became a beautiful place to live again. Kids were running the streets and parents weren't worried. The neighbors began bringing the vegetable stands back out, and they even seemed to taste better, as if the Blackhand's presence in the area was no longer tainting the soil. The fire at Talapini's house could be seen for miles, as it sat at the top of a hill. The flames illuminated the sky that night, and as the neighbor's woke, to see their windows glowing orange, everyone knew whose home it was. Nobody seemed in much of a hurry to help though, they just stare out the window and imagine the possibilities of what was to come.

Three weeks go by, Yano finally awakens to see nothing but hospital walls. Yano tries to move around in bed but is stopped, his hands are both secured to the railings. Not for or by any hospital measures, but by the police. Yano is handcuffed. This is the moment that he has dreaded, being caught. Now what happens, he thought. Horror stories created by his mind about prison life started running through his head, playing out multiple scenarios. Is he going to go away for life? Will he be killed inside? The Blackhand surely has a reach on the inside of the prison walls.

As Yano lay in bed feeling sorry for himself, the door opens. His mother, Fina, walks in. She is crying and cannot believe what was happening. She was forced to work almost every hour of the day in order to pay bills, put food on their table, and pay the Blackhand the money in which Enzo could not pay. She had no time to even notice that her sons were acting in any way suspicious, or murderous. The news of everything that has happened hit her like a brick wall, like the brick wall had a loose brick that somebody tugged on, and the rest of the wall tumbled down on top of her.

"By yourself?" she asked.

"What do you mean Mama?"

"Did you do this by yourself or was your brother involved?"

"I don't understand mama, I didn't do anything. This is all a setup. I…"

Before he could finish his lie, Fina's open palm landed on Yano's cheek harder than ever before.

"I understand the need to do what you did, Yano, but going through with it and involving your brother, it is disgraceful."

"Mama, I had to do it. I couldn't let them get away with what they did to father. It wasn't going to end. If I just let them walk away and they did to someone else what they did to father, his death would be on my conscience."

"So turning to murder is justified?"

"In my eyes? Yes."

"What is the Lord going to say to you on judgment day, Yano?"

"I don't care, mama. Doesn't the bible say an eye for an eye?"

"Yano, these are stories to help us understand the true way of living, they are not meant to take literally. The bible does say that. You're right. It also says to love thy neighbor, it says to turn the other cheek, it says multiple things that contradict revenge."

"I'm sorry, mama, but I couldn't stand seeing them walk the streets of our neighborhood anymore. To see them stand right where my father was killed and laugh and enjoy their life without precautions. Punishment had to be handed out."

"Yano! Judgment is not your lace. The Lord tells us, judge not lest ye be judged, remember? No man has the right to judge another for his actions, and you do not have any say so in that man's punishment or pennants to God."

Fina lived her life by the word of the Bible. She was understanding how Yano had the urge to avenge his father but disappointed in the fact that he turned thought into action. She bends over and kisses her eldest child on the forehead and whispers,

"May God have mercy on your soul child."

As Fina turns to walk out, Yano watches her. His heartbroken knowing that he disappointed his mother, to see her in tears and such sorrow, and know that it is his fault. He begins to cry as the door shuts behind her, knowing that this may be the last time he ever sees or speaks with his mother.

Yano stays in the hospital for two more weeks while his recovery is made and then they take him to the courthouse for sentencing. The judge could only prove that Yano was at Talapini's home that night. He did not shoot at any police officer, so their deaths were not laid at Yano's feet. When his bullet-riddled body was taken to the hospital, there was no weapon near him. Charging him with murder was almost impossible, but charging him with conspiracy to murder multiple people was not. Yano was sentenced to twenty years in prison, and eligible for parole after ten years.

While Yano is adjusting to his new life, Gino tries to settle into his. He begins going back to school. Afterward, he stays at home with Rosaria. This eliminates the need for a babysitter and takes some of the stress off of Fina. He falls into a deep state of depression after losing his brother, he doesn't want to do anything. School only lasts for a few weeks before he stops getting up in the morning all together. The Blackhand is almost finished in the neighborhood, so the enforcers who come to collect do not come around much anymore. Fina still chooses to work long hours, not needing as much money is of no concern to her, though keeping her mind occupied from the fact that she lost another family member is.

Yano leaves the courthouse with his head high. Though distraught, and almost broken, he didn't want to seem so. Even as he entered prison, he was afraid. Afraid of what may happen, afraid of retaliation at home and leaving Gino alone. Yano has faced many obstacles over the last few years and was able to overcome them while facing incredible odds at times, though does that mean anything in here? Are the things that he has been through considered child's play compared to what happens in prison, or will he be looked upon as someone who is not to be messed with? Yano's mind is racing the entire time he walks down this long hallway. Lights flickering, a damp smell, a muggy feeling, spiderwebs everywhere. The place seemed to be falling apart.

The floor of the hall is unlevel, bricks sticking up here and there, Yano trips a few times. This does not throw off his concentration. As he enters the main prison and sees the cell block, he cannot believe how many inmates are there. There are twenty-six cells on each level with a total of eight levels. This was just Yano's section of the prison. With two men to a cell that equaled over four hundred inmates that Yano had to watch. This seems almost impossible for him. For a twenty-year-old kid, living in a two-bedroom room the size of a large closet, this is a big change for him. He is nervous as he sits on his cot looking at his cellmate, though very willing to do anything he has to in order to survive. He has proven that to himself time and time again in recent years.

Once the guards finished explaining the rules to Yano, they shut the cell door and walked away. Yano and his cellmate's eyes were locked in a familiar feeling. Was it the situation that was familiar to Yano, or this man's face? He couldn't tell. Yano was preparing himself mentally for what was to come as the second man stands from his bed. Yano stands, with both of them now standing, with only a toilets width between the two, they stare at each other suspenseful. Yano thinks, should I make the first move or is he just sizing me up? The second guy slightly nods his head a few times and lays back down without a word spoken. He picks up his book and tends to his affairs. Yano then turns and looks out of the cell door. He is high up, not on the eight-level, but certainly not on the main. The fourth, so he thinks. He turns back around and looks at his new home. If he were to take six, maybe seven, regularly sized steps he would be on the other side. If he lifts both arms, fingertips on each hand are about a foot from touching each wall.

Yano can barely take it all in, the loss of freedom is the loss of everything. He can no longer even use the toilet in private, this is the most wretched situation he has ever been in.

The next morning comes, and guards are yelling for everyone to wake up. Yano wakes but doesn't get out from under the itchy wool blanket.

"Better get up Yano," says the roommate.

"Guards don't care much for guys who ignore morning or night time count."

"Count?"

"Ya, the guards come around each morning to count the inmates. They have to make sure that there is the same number here in the morning that was here at night. You know? In case someone escaped."

"Escape? Does that happen a lot? I mean, is it even possible?"

Yano looks around at the stone walls, stone ceiling, and iron bars in the window.

"Oh it's very possible, but no, it doesn't happen often. Just get the fuck up already. They're almost here."

Yano stands up and slips on his shoes, and stands next to his cellmate.

"How do you know my name?"

His cellmate smiles and shhh's him as the guards get to their cell. Yano stares at the guy cautiously as the guards step in front of their door and count off.

"One, Two."

The second guy turns to Yano,

"You don't have any idea who I am, do you?"

"Should I?"

"Well considering we're from the same neighborhood, ya, I would expect you to recognize me. It has been a while since we saw each other though, and I guess I may have changed a little, so it's ok."

Yano couldn't be more confused right now. As he stares back, he gives in to Yano's confusion.

"Antonio….Marducci."

"Sounds familiar."

"Ya, I'm friends with your brother, Gino. I killed that guy in the Blackhand years ago for fuckin' with him."

"The one who killed his little Irish friend?"

"Ya. Patty. That was horrible, he was a good kid."

"Ok I remember you now, you were a lot younger then."

"Ya, the same age as Gino."

"How much time did you get?"

"Ten years. Could've been paroled at five, but my behavior in here ain't been that good. Pretty hard to be a good citizen in this place, ya know?"

"No I don't know, but I imagine I'll find out pretty quick."

"Ya, you probably will," Antonio chuckles.

"Though, from what I remember, you should do alright."

"And what is it that you remember?"

"Spilotti."

"What do you know about that?"

"Man, the entire neighborhood knew about that."

Yano looks at Antonio, a bit confused as to how anyone else knew.

"You weren't very sly, Yano. Probably your first kill though right?"

Yano just nods.

"Ya, I figured. Man, you were seen standing outside his house with Dino, entering his house through the window or some shit. Then he left in a hurry and he ended up waking up dead the next day. Not hard for them witnesses to put the clues together."

"So, if people knew, why didn't anyone ever say anything?"

"What? Lock you up for killing the man that everyone was afraid of? Na, people were happy. Everyone knew that bad shit was going to come from it, but it had to happen. The Blackhand wasn't just going to walk away. So… did you kill them all?"

"Almost. Well, I don't even know. We killed most of them, if not all."

"So what put you in here?"

"Arsen."

"Damn, that's a serious charge."

"I wasn't charged with it, that's just what put me in here. I burned down Don Talapini's house, forcing everyone outside. Then we killed as many escapees as we could. Cops must've seen the blaze."

Ya, haha, or heard the gunshots!"

Yano and Antonio sit talking about the events that happened. Yano was not the type to just give his trust away, though Gino always spoke highly of Antonio. The fact that Yano and his friends had one less man to kill because Antonio took him out helped also. Antonio says how people love him inside the walls because of his crime, so Yano should have no worries.

"So you're saying that I have absolutely nothing to worry about?"

"Well, no. Not for sure, nobody knows nothing in here for sure. Not even the guards. Only the shot-callers know anything because nothing happens without their say so. I'm just saying, multiple murders, people are going to fear you, at the very least, respect the shit out of you."

Yano looks at Antonio and realizes that he is a friend, though his demeanor is not what Yano wants to be affiliated with. Yano wants to be a respectable businessman who is feared just as much.

"You need to respect yourself more."

"What the fuck are you talkin' about Yano?"

"How do you expect to get respect from others when you don't even respect yourself?"

"I don't give a shit about them respecting me, I only care about being feared."

"Respect is just as good as fear."

"How do you figure?"

"Fear is what you want your enemy to have, but your friends? Do you want them to fear you also? If your friends do what you ask out of fear and not respect, are they your friends?"

"Ok, I think I get your point."

"You don't have to swear so much to get your point across. I use that language at times, but we need to portray ourselves as people of higher intelligence than these other fools in here. We don't want to give off the impression that we're uneducated, hoodlums."

"hahaha, but we *are* uneducated. Hoodlums is exactly what we are, not only that but now we're also felons, in prison."

"Yes, but we don't have to act like it. We have the time to get educated, and just because we have a street background, doesn't mean our future has to stay the same. Also, I'm not just an ordinary street guy, so watch how you speak to me."

Yano explains how he made a difference in the neighborhood. He has friends, and the people in the neighborhood are grateful for the outcome of his actions. Many of them spoke at his trial which is what got Yano a reduced sentence of ten years instead of thirty. His friends are going to keep the neighborhood in line so it stays a safe place.

"When I get out, things will be different."

"Ya, Yano, that's ten to twenty years from now. The only thing that you need to be worried about in here, is making friends *in here*, the outside means nothing to us anymore."

A New Plan

YANO IS FRESH off of the streets. Fresh off of a bloody vendetta that lasted a long time. He worked with three other guys who were not afraid of saying how they feel or coming up with murderous plots. Yano can tell that look that one gets when they are thinking of something evil. Antonio has plans, and Yano can see it.

"What are you thinking, Antonio?"

"You say we have plenty of time to get educated right? Well, I say that we have plenty of time to do other things also."

"Get to your point already."

"The white boys and the blacks run this place. Everything is either white or black, there is no in-between, there is nobody else. People like us have to look over our shoulder while walking the yard all the time and I'm tired of it."

"People like us?"

"Italian. Not white, not black. Were targets by the blacks because we look white, and targeted by the whites because they know that we're not one of them. We have nothing, its like every Italian for himself in here."

"So you want to start attacking blacks and whites? How is that going to help us?"

"No Yano, can't you see? We have huge numbers here but we have no organization. Most whites in here are in here for violent crimes against blacks, and vice versa with the blacks. Italians, well most of us here, are not violent by nature. They need to be taught, they need to learn survival skills, we need leadership."

Yano looks at the ceiling, half-listening, half dozing off. He hasn't been harassed yet, by anyone, so he doesn't quite understand the need for what Antonio is talking about yet.

"These damn Aryans and the Zulu Nation run this place and I hate it. At the very least, we need to be powerful enough to protect ourselves. We need to unite, create some sort of brotherhood."

Yano is beginning to get his point.

"Niggers and peckerwoods need to learn respect for us and stop treatin' us like a bunch of dumbass immigrants."

"Stop with that sort of language, what did I tell you? I don't care how much you hate someone, do not let them hear you speak like that. You have always got to remain calm and civilized. This way nobody, friend or foe, will know what you're thinking. If you let them know what you're thinking then you have no element of surprise."

Yano is demanding respect from Antonio while trying to make him respect himself. He needs people on his side who can be trusted, not someone who is going to be unpredictable.

Later that night, Yano was introduced to Vinnie Marino. Vinnie was already one year into a five-year sentence for a botched jewelry heist. Vinnie is a twenty-five-year-old guy from Chicago. He was up in Omaha visiting family when he got mixed up in a job. The guy who was with him was caught and turned rat on Vinnie. The guy walked with a few month's probation while Vinnie got a long stretch.

Antonio spoke of Yano to Vinnie before, before Yano arrived even, so Vinnie knows what type of guy Yano is and that he is from the Omaha area. He was excited to meet Yano because he had to ask a favor.

"Yano, Antonio has talked about you. You seem like a guy who can be trusted. I need to ask a favor of you."

"I don't even know you. What makes you think that I would be willing to do you any favors?"

"Because you're new here, and you're going to need a favor eventually. Friends are hard to come by in the joint."

Yano agrees to hear Vinnie out but wasn't guaranteeing anything.

"The guy who put me away. He lives in your neighborhood."

"So?"

"So, I need you to take him out. It's going to be years before I'm out of here and who knows where that cock sucker will be by then. I'll probably never find him, and he needs to get what he deserves, fuckin' rat."

"I don't know if you noticed, but I'm in here too. It's going to be even longer for me to get out. What exactly do you want me to do?"

"Your brother, Gino. He could do it for me."

"I don't know. I don't like the idea of putting my brother in that kind of situation while I'm not there to watch his back."

"What about Angelo then?' asked Antonio.

Yano shook his head in despair. He doesn't like this, he doesn't even know how to get the word out to them. Nobody has come for a visit yet, and he cannot call Dino due to him also being a felon.

"I'll see what I can do, I guess."

"I owe you big, Yano. Thank you."

Yano and Antonio sat around in their cell with Vinnie and began to talk about new plans for the Italian and Sicilian people in the prison. A new future for their people. A time to give their people hope instead of fear. A time for them to become feared instead of being afraid. The whites and the blacks have a war that's been going on forever and the Italians are just kind of stuck in the middle, but no more.

Meanwhile, back at home, certain things changed while others remained the same. Dino went back to putting all of his concentration on running his games. Gino left school and began to feel as if something in his life was missing. His thrill was gone. He became addicted to the life his brother and he began and going straight again was proving near impossible. Angelo fell upon the idea of selling stolen goods, mainly petty items, rings, and watches at first. He then graduated from hijacking trucks. Trucks full of dresses, fur coats, and suits. These items were easier to move than jewelry because people bought in bulk. Angie stole loads and sold them to the same stores that ordered them for a discounted price. The store owners got cheaper goods which meant more profit while the distribution companies collected the insurance money. Everybody was winning. The three former vendetta killers still spoke on almost a regular basis. Over the past years, they built a bond that couldn't be broken.

Fina has been able to save up some extra money in recent months. Not needing to pay any corrupt organization has saved her a lot of money and stress. She no longer needs to work long hours, though she still chooses to. Being at home, seeing what she has only reminded her of what she lost, Enzo, and Yano. She loved her job and didn't mind being there. She had a good, trustworthy, neighborhood friend who would walk Rosaria to school in the morning as well as pick her up. Fina worked until the sun went down, so her daughter pretty much lived with this friend. She would go home in time to kiss her mama goodnight and then go to sleep.

Fina was able to get enough cash put together for her and her two remaining, unincarcerated, children to go visit their brother. Gino was thrilled. It has been almost six months since he has seen Yano in that hospital bed, and even then, he was asleep so they didn't get the chance to speak. Fina still had to wait another couple of weeks to get some downtime at work so she didn't leave her boss shorthanded. As a natural-born citizen, from a family of generations of natural-born citizens, he didn't quite care for immigrants and had no corals with replacing one. Fina had no choice but to wait until he said she could go.

Fina begged her boss but got nowhere. She didn't attempt to pursue the matter too strongly because she knew that her job could easily be taken from her. Then what would she do? She doesn't know how to do anything else. She loved speaking with the new Italians coming in through the same train that she was on just a few short years earlier. Hearing the stories of home, of their travels, of their expectations of the new world reminded her of herself and Enzo. She is constantly reminded of how excited her family was to come here, to America. The land of the free, where dreams are not born, but where they come true. She is then reminded, at times, of how coming here was not such a good thing for her family. She speaks not of her troubles to the new arrivals, she just listens and thinks of happier times.

The Visit

GINO WAS AWAKE all night. There was too much excitement running through him to sleep. His brain and body had no way of relaxing. He was up as soon as the sun was, making breakfast for his mother and sister. As Fina and Rosaria awoke, they ate, and Gino was rushing them out of the door.

"Gino! I need to take a shower and get ready!" said Fina.

"No you don't, you look fine. Let's get going."

"The visiting times do not even start for three more hours and it's a two-hour drive, so we have time. Relax."

Gino did not like hearing that. He wanted to get there as early as possible. Without even a word from Yano in the past six months, the family had no idea how Yano was doing. Gino has only a memory of a father, and now also lost his only brother. He cannot wait to see him, his patients have been very thin ever since Fina told him of this visit.

That same morning, Yano was awakened by a guard calling his name, among many others.

"What's he talking about?" Yano asked Antonio.

"Its visitation day," Antonio replied.

"I don't get visits. Why is he calling my name?"

"I don't know. You must be getting one today."

Yano rose from his cement slab of a bed and began to urinate in the toilet that was just as close to his bed as his pillow was. He then decided to go take a shower, just in case he was indeed getting visitors today. As Yano entered the shower room (twenty-four showerheads in total, eight along each long wall and four along each shorter wall, with no privacy walls in between) he undressed and turned the water on. Before the water could reach a temperature that Yano was comfortable with, a big man came from behind. This man shoved Yano up against the wall. Two huge black arms wrapped around Yano's head and neck, attempting to choke him.

In the free world, a few months before this attack, a black man was roughed up by some Italians. This man was beaten and put in the hospital where he later died. The guy attacking Yano was this dead man's cousin. He had recently found out that Yano is from the same approximate location as his cousin's assault and was not in prison at the time. He decided to take his revenge on Yano with the assumption that he was involved in his cousin's murder somehow.

Yano is almost beat, he can hardly breathe at this point. He can summon one last burst of strength as he puts his foot up against the wall and pushes himself backward. The assailant falls back and pulls Yano to the floor with him. As the two men hit the floor, the man drops a sharp piece of metal. Yano sees this and struggles to break free of the man's grip. The two guys wrestle around on the wet shower floor for what seemed like an eternity, though in reality, it was probably only a few short minutes. When your fighting for your life, time ceases to exist, one minute can feel like twenty.

Yano thrusts his head backward and hits the guy in the nose. The man's grip loosens and Yano is finally able to slip free. Yano lunges to his side and grabs the homemade weapon. He turns back toward the man, climbs up on top of him, puts one hand over his mouth to muffle the screams. He then sticks the metal in between the man's ribs, pulls it out, and then replaces it. The hand wielding the weapon begins to move in a circular motion, spinning the blade and ripping everything that came in to contact with it inside him. The eyes of the two are locked. Yano does not know who this man is, but he *does* want him to die. Yano stands back up and washes the blood off of him, gets dressed, and leaves the room while the man lays there bleeding out.

As Yano walks away from the shower room, he is smiling. He cannot believe that that just happened. He cannot believe that he was able to get free from that man's intense grip and reverse the roles of the would-be assassin's original plan. He could not believe that nobody else walked in. Several different outcomes could have happened, though none of them did. After six months inside, Yano was finally tested, and he passed. He won. He was not worried about being caught, not worried about the repercussions that would surely occur when the Zulu Nation hears of a dead brother. He missed this, the killing, the watching of a man's soul as it leaves the body, taking life away. No, he did not worry about a thing, he doesn't even look behind to see if anybody witnessed him leaving the area, he simply smiles as he walks back to his cell and awaits the guards to take him to his visit.

As Yano finally gets to see his family again, he is greeted with tears and frustration. Tears from his mother and sister, but frustration from his brother. Gino does nothing but speaks on how he is going to move on their enemies. Yano, being incarcerated and far away from being able to protect Gino, does not like this.

"You need to wait until I'm out Gino."

"Why?"

"So I can be there to help you."

"I'll be ok. Dino and Angelo are with me. I'll be ok."

Yano can see that nothing he says will stop Gino, and nothing Gino says will comfort Yano. He is going to do whatever he wants to do, regardless of where Yano is.

"At least do me one favor," Yano asks. "Keep me in the loop. Come visit me, explain to me what is happening and what your plans are. Let me help with what I can, please."

Gino gives his brother a slight nod. This is not what Yano wants from his brother at all, but this way, at least his actions on the streets will not be completely unknown. Gino is given the task set up by Vinnie, and as he nods to Yano, he is excited. Excited to get back into the life, and excited to be helping out his big brother again.

The Beginning Of The End

B Y NOON THE following day, there wasn't an inmate in the prison who hadn't heard about the dead guy found in the shower. The blacks inmates were in an uproar as they scoured the yard seeking answers. The white boys questioned every member, also trying to find out who did it. They also stood up for the Italians at times (when they could benefit from it) so they approached them as well. The white boys ran a gambling ring and pimped out weaker inmates, while the blacks controlled the drugs. Each wanted what the other had and, at times, have tried to take it. The blacks automatically assumed it was a white boy who attacked them. Who else? Why would an Italian do it? They're not organized, if one of them did do it, then it had to be on orders from the peckerwoods, or so they thought.

The leaders of the Black Nation kept thinking could this be the whites trying to make another move on their drug trade? They sat back and began to plan a retaliation. If their drug trade is under siege then they must fight back in order to protect it. As the situation remained unsolved, the blacks and whites both on edge, preparing for war, Yano sits back and watches. "These guys are always fighting right?" Yano asked Antonio. As Antonio nodded yes, Yano continues. "Well, as they fight their next inevitable war, we will organize. We will begin to build an organization bigger than either of them and more powerful. By the time they have almost completely wiped each other out, we will be ready to slide in and take over everything. Drugs and gambling both. Prostitution will be eradicated. We will not only stand for ourselves, but for those who cannot stand for themselves, Italian, black, or white. Any Italian that does not join us is on his own. Pass the word around. The time of the Italian underdog is over." Yano walks back to his cell, leaving Antonio standing there alone, with a smile.

Later that night, a couple of black men approached Yano's cell. They demanded answers from Yano. Yano, unafraid, stands up and looks them right in the face. "I was going to let you and the white boys fight this out as you blamed them for the murder. However, since you come asking me about it, I must tell you the truth. I am no liar, my word is the truth and I honor any words that come from my mouth." Yano walks closer to the men, "I killed that guy." The angry men glance at each other in disbelief. Yano is alone but admits to an offense that may very well get him killed. Yano explains the situation and how it was nothing against the black population. He was only fighting to save his life. It was a personal beef between the two. After all, was said and done, one man spoke to Yano, explaining that the hit against him was unsanctioned by the Nation. They assured Yano if he was speaking the truth about it being personal between the two men, then the Nation would back off of Yano.

"We need to be completely sure that what you say isn't bull shit and that you aren't planning anything else."

Yano looks at the man, "I told you, I am no liar. I am no coward and I am not afraid of any of you, so what would I gain by lying?"

"Well, we're going to back off seeing as how this was not a Nation call. By backing off, I mean that we won't completely crush you and every other Italian in this place, though we are going to need some sort of payment for your very disrespectful offense."

"Disrespectful offense? That man rushed me in the shower, pulled a weapon on me. I did what I had to do."

"We understand all of that," says a second Nation member, "however, he was connected, protected. You killed one of ours. No matter what the circumstances, we have to retaliate. Not to do so makes us look weak."

Yano nods at the men, "Do what you have to do."

Standing there, holding his ground against multiple assailants, Yano was prepared for punishment. His fists begin to ball up, he prepares himself mentally for a fight. The men look at him,

"We'll let you know what we decide."

"I'll be waiting."

"Who the fuck are you? Ain't nobody in here ever heard of you on the streets, yet you have the balls to stand here and speak to us like you're some kind of street soldier."

"I have never heard of you either. Does that mean I shouldn't be afraid of what you are willing to do?" Yano replies.

"My name is Marty Smith. I run shit in here."

Before he could finish, Yano interrupts, "No. You run black shit in here. You have no say over myself, or any other Italian in here."

"Hahaha, you really do have some big fuckin' balls kid. Watch your back. You owe us a debt, and we will come collecting someday."

As Marty and his thugs stand there threatening Yano, they are completely unaware of the white boys that approach from both sides.

"These fuckin' monkeys bothering you kid?"

"Na, we're good."

Marty looks around, turns back to Yano, and nods his head. As he turns to walk away, he lifts his hand and with one long finger, points at Yano and smiles.

"Hey, hold on a second," Yano says, and as Marty turns back around, Yano spills the beans.

"Bussiness in here is going to be conducted a little different from now on. I am setting a tax, twenty-five percent of all weekly drug sales."

Marty, a forty-seven-year-old man, grey hair, wrinkled face, begins to laugh. Marty has been incarcerated for over fifteen years, he won't give in to Yano without a fight.

"Payments are due every Monday, starting next week. If no payment is made, I will take it as a sign of disrespect, and then bodies will begin to fall. No signs, no warnings, no second chances. Monday by lunchtime, green money in my hand, or blacks bodies on the floor. Your choice."

Yano turns and walks back to his bunk.

"You can't be fuckin' serious! You damn dago, you think you're going to threaten me, my business, my men?"

"Monday, by lunch, or coons will hit the floor in record numbers."

Marty was extremely pissed. He turns and walks away, but not with any intent on paying Yano.

"We need to take him out," Marty says to his guys.

The white boys laugh as one says, "I can't believe you're going to tax the nig..."

Before he could finish Yano says, "Not just him. I am also taking a percentage of your business."

They all laugh and walk away without even acknowledging his statement.

Yano, also smiling, sits back and begins to figure out his next move. Without completely thinking this plan through, he had already set it in motion. The long term outcome is clear, but the choices and consequences of his actions getting there are still hazy. Vinnie and Antonio are let in on what had happened. They are both eager to begin building an Italian rule in prison, but they both are also aware that Yano may have played his cards too early. They have yet to begin organizing their people, yet Yano has already begun threatening the competition and creating rivals. They have to work fast. The two begin speaking with as many Italians as possible, trying to recruit. If you are not with us, then you're against us, which is the slogan they decide to use. Intimidation, surprisingly, is not a tool that they had to use as often as they thought. Most Italian and Sicilian inmates were quite reluctant to join up. Every one of them agreeing to all terms, they each report to a boss, their boss also reports to another boss, and that boss gets orders directly from Yano. Not one Italian is allowed to do whatever he wants, not allowed to speak with Yano. Some kind of order has to be built and the order has to be maintained.

Yano will have Vinnie and Antonio underneath him. These will be Yano's confidants, the ones who help him with all the business and plans. Both Vinnie and Antonio will have a few men underneath them who they keep in contact with, and those men will control all of the rest of the men. The organization built up pretty quick, with Yano right on top. As of this moment, the idea of organizing was purely theoretical. The desires of each Italian inmate would need to be tested. Talking about building and acting on the building process is different. Is everyone going to be able to do what needs to be done? Yano has his doubts but there is no way to tell yet. The theoretical must be put into practice.

"You both know that the blacks are going to come for me, right?" Yano asks his two underlings.

Vinnie and Antonio both agree, what Yano did was stupid. He put the cart before the horse. They both also understand why he did it. If there is going to be a time to stand your ground and begin to build their own thing, that was the time. Yano accepted responsibility for killing that man, without lying, without fear of retaliation. This showed the enemy that Yano is fearless. He had to do it, regardless of how many followers he did or did not have at that time. To show weakness there, or any other time, there is no coming back from that. Yano had to play the cards he was dealt, and now he needs to capitalize on it before the Black Nation does.

"So," Vinnie starts, "Are we going to set up a hit right now? I have guys who are ready to pop off."

"No. I told them they had until Monday."

"Yano, they're not going to pay you and they're not going to wait until Monday to let you know. They're going to move on you quick."

"We have to be men of our word. We have to make the point that what we say, we mean. Our language as to be feared as much as our actions."

Yano knows that waiting is stupid, it's reckless. The Zulu retaliation will probably come sooner. Yano still waits. Over the four days that they wait, three Italian men are found dead. One killed in the shower, which must have had to have some sort of symbolic meaning. Yano killed a man, and started this feud, in the shower. There is no way that this was not a message. The second two were both killed out in the yard. They all know what is happening, and Yano's followers are becoming a bit nervous. Some even begin to question Yano's ability to run this organization. Yano is upset about the deaths as well, yet he feels that making his point is more important than being sucked into an average prison yard war.

"We have to be smarter than them," he says.

"We need action!" Vinnie responds. "Our followers are not going to be following us anymore if we do not start acting Yano."

Antonio seems to feel the same as everyone else, yet does not speak on it. He knows about the things that Yano did back in the neighborhood, he knows Yano is no coward, yet he is confused as to why Yano is waiting. As everyone else begins to doubt Yano, Antonio just wishes he would act already and prove everyone wrong. Prove to Antonio that he is still the same guy from the T.K.B. that turned murderous in the neighborhood. The same guy that caused enemies to fill their streets and cause Antonio to be put in this hell hole.

Power Play

SUNDAY HAS ARRIVED. Sunday night, a meeting was held, plans were made. Monday came. Nerves are on edge. Marty Smith had no plans to pay Yano and Yano knew that. No payment of any kind came Yano's way. All-day, Yano waited. Nothing. As dinner time rolls around, plans were about to be put into action. The action that everyone was waiting for, yet nobody expected. Yano's orders were given, as they were acted upon, events unfolded in a way that nobody in this prison, even the guards, has ever seen before. As the clock struck 7:00, attacks all over the prison happened simultaneously.

In the cafeteria, a few black men were jumped, stabbed with utensils, and beaten with metal dinner trays until dead. Out in the yard, men were stabbed, in the shower men were found were throats slit from ear to ear. Two men had their skulls crushed by weights in the exercise area. All over the prison, twenty of Smith's top men were put on display as their lives were savagely stolen. Yano also added another piece to his plan. These twenty men were a part of his message that he is someone to fear. However, the three Italians that had been killed during the waiting process had to be avenged. Yano sent six men to the area that Smith was at. They hit fast and they hit hard. Before Smith and his guys even saw it coming, three more black men lay dead on the floor, and Smith has a knife sticking from his shoulder.

"Your life is to be spared … for now." One assailant whispered to Marty as he drove his piece of metal into his body. "But this puts you behind one payment. Better be more prepared when the next one comes due."

Alarms began to chime out throughout the prison air, guards were being dispersed everywhere. The attacks were so randomly placed that the guards were not sure of where to go next to prevent any more death from happening. All that could be done was to round up all prisoners and lock them back into their cells. Italian inmates throughout all cell blocks were proud, Blacks were confused and upset, Whites laughed as they tried not to figure out what had happened, but revel in the spilling of so much Black blood. As for the guards, well they were perplexed, they were in a state of utter disbelief that something like this could have happened without any warning.

When all was done and everything starts to calm down, Smith begins to plan out his next move. Though he does not quite realize that Yano's plans are still not finished.

Smith is mad. Lying in bed recovering from the shoulder wound, he thinks. How could this have happened and how could Yano have pulled it off? He doesn't understand any of it. Yano hasn't even been locked up long enough to figure out who his top guys are, yet almost every one of them was murdered within five minutes of each other, scattered throughout the facility. This, in Smith's mind, is too complex of a plan for a simple-minded Italian ghetto boy to conceive.

"Those white boys really fucked you guys up today I heard," a voice from behind the wall says.

"Who the fuck are you?" Smith hollers back.

"Just a bystander."

"Well, mind your fuckin business."

As Smith tries to ignore the voice from the neighboring cell, he couldn't help but wonder why this faceless man thinks it was the whites who attacked the Nation.

"White boys?"

"Yep," the man replies.

"You may have heard wrong, those damn crackers aren't smart enough to pull off something like this."

"Oh, and who is then? The Italians?" the man giggles.

"Get to the fuckin point."

"No point, just stating an observation, I thought I could kick up a bit of conversation."

"Oh, are we fuckin friends now?"

"Why not? Everyone can use a friend."

"Well, friend, you're wrong. The white boys ain't pull this shit and I don't know how those uneducated immigrant Italian pricks could have done this."

"It's because they didn't. The white boys did."

"You got something to say, fuckin say it already!"

"well, from what I heard, the white boys overheard your altercation somewhere with an Italian guy and decided to use this as an excuse to jump."

"Why would they do that? Why would they hide behind an unorganized group of wops?"

"Because. It's a smart idea. They get you guys to attack the Italians while they sneak behind you and steal the drug trade from you."

Smith takes all of this new news into consideration, besides, it makes sense. The white boys were there when Yano threatened a tax on the Nation, so their rising conflict was of no secret. Is this why three Italians were killed and no visible retaliation occurred?

"What's your name, friend?"

"Lou. Lou Bistone."

"Italian?"

"Ya but not with Yano."

"A loner huh?"

"Yep, a lone shark swimming in a dirty ass ocean."

"Well, friend, I think that you could be of some use to me."

Lou grins as he realizes that his newfound friendship has taken root. Protection from the blacks against the whites is what he needs, and protection from the Italians is what he wants Smith to believe he seeks. Yano had put this pawn into play. A red herring to distract Smith from what's to come. Lou will be placed beside Smith as he tries to rebuild, feeding him false information that Yano tells him. Smith falls for the bait, but still hesitant, brings Lou close to him, thinking that having an Italian in his pocket could prove useful against Yano. A double agent, but in all actuality, he would be a triple agent, undercover as a snitch for the Italians pretending to be undercover and snitching for the blacks. This is a tough cover to keep, but his only job. He will never have contact with Yano, not even with Vinnie or Antonio, but one of the lower underlings, so no suspicion should ever arise.

Lou fed Smith information that causes Smith to organize a hit against the white boys. Fifteen of the top members are sought out and treated as pin cushions. Now the white boys are pissed, and a war between them and the Nation is inevitable. Yano's plan is beginning to take shape. He knew that the blacks would never agree to any type of tax, though he does ultimately intend on taking it. Within a few days after Yano's initial hit, there lay almost fifty people, black, white, and Italian, dead on the floor. The war is on, and the prison goes into lockdown.

This did not stop the war. Food poisoning killed inmates, radio explosions began to occur, cells were lit on fire. The guards could not stop it. Inmates had to be allowed to cook the meals and contaminating specific trays was not hard. The inmates were also in charge of delivering books to cells. Walking by and spraying flammable cleaning supplies with a lit match became quite popular. Guards were seriously undermanned and had no choice but to have inmates do these jobs, so opportunities would always arise.

Year Three

THREE YEARS OF incarceration, one single visit, an undying war, and the pain of lost love is all that Yano has, besides being the boss of an organization that has become the most violent group that any prison guard has ever seen. Arabella. The beautiful girl from down the street. This girl still haunts Yano's dreams nightly. The letters have almost stopped coming entirely, yet when they do, they are of no true purpose. Having an almost obligatory feeling towards them. The hole in Yano's heart for this girl will never heal, yet he does not dare to tell her this. Having the courage to pull a man's eyeball from his head with his soup spoon comes naturally these days, but telling his feelings to the one constant love that he has is near impossible. Someday he plans to tell her, someday he plans to write, but it is not this day. No, this day, like all of the others, he chooses to simply lie back and reminisce on her beauty.

A girl who he once thought that he would spend the rest of his days with, raise a family, and grow old with, no longer shows affection in her letters. Easy to understand that the letters would simply be carbon copies of the previous if the kept going the way that they started. It has been three years, there's only so many ways to say that you love a person. The letters dwindled to almost nothing, common courtesy letters. His were of a mirror image back to her. No longer signing with loving words, no longer describing the pain each felt from being away from the other. These correspondences became simple formalities to remind each other that they are still there. Thoughts, hopes, and dreams from what seems to be another life are of no concern to Yano anymore. No matter how strong his long continues to be for Arabella, while he is on the inside, his mind must remain clear. One day he will be free and they will have the chance to reconnect if she is still around.

As the third year of Yano's sentence is underway, the war rages on. The Nation is hurting, suffering dozens of fatalities. The white boys are passed hurting, they are struggling to survive. Between the Nation and the Italians attacking from both fronts, the white boys are at an all-time low, but with the number of inmates that they have coming in each year they are not even close to being completely wiped out. Just out of talent. The recruits fight to stay alive but have no clue what their organization is all about, they are sucked into the middle of something that they will never understand. The Nation also has new inmates coming in by the dozens, not as many as the white gang, but more than the Italians. Being Italian means playing smart, their numbers do not get replenished as fast as the enemies so staying off of the front lines and attacking from the side is what is needed to be done.

During lunchtime, in the cafeteria, as Yano walks in, a fight breaks out. Antonio and Vinnie quickly jump in front of Yano to keep him safe. As they back out of the battlefield the guards come rushing in. Men are stacked on top of each other, arms flailing wildly. It is to hard to see who is who, who is on top, who is on the bottom, the only thing for sure is that someone is bleeding. As the guards start at the top of the pile, pulling and throwing the inmates to the side, they eventually make it to the bottom. With all of this noise, only one man lay dead. Lou Bistone. Yano's undercover snitch in the Nation's ranks has been murdered. Lou was a key player in the Italian organization (which they now refer to as 'the family') and a very important aspect in keeping the Blacks in line for Yano. None of the men attacking him were of any color, just white. The Nation didn't do this, but why would the white boys? Granted that they were all at war with each other but hitting Lou seems suspicious. Was he a victim of a random attack or did the white boys finally realize that Lou is the one who blamed the initial attack on them? If they did find out about Lou's position, then they must surely know that Yano put him in play.

Yano has but one idea left. He wants no more Italian blood spilled. The war must end. Yano decides to approach Smith for a sit-down. With four muscular guards around, Smith sits at the table. Yano walks up with only Antonio and Vinnie at his side. He sits, knowing that Smith considered Lou an asset to information, though false, about the Italians. He would be just as upset by his death as Yano is.

"I have a proposition for you," Yano begins.

Smith says nothing, just stares Yano in the eye.

"I want this war to be over."

Smith lets out a sigh of relief, nods, and responds, "What brings this about?"

"I am tired of the blood. To many Italians have lost their lives."

"Too many of my people also,"

"I do not care about your people. If I could continue this war with a guarantee that Italian blood would no longer spill, then I would wipe you out completely Marty."

"Hmm, so why now? What is this deal you say you have?"

"I will lower my request of twenty-five percent to fifteen."

"Ten" Smith replies.

Smith wants to pay nothing, but this war is interrupting business. Losing ten percent is better than losing the almost eighty percent that has been lost during their feud.

"I will consider ten. I need something from you though."

Marty lifts both hands, giving a gesture as if to say 'what would that be'.

"The white brotherhood, they need to go away."

"Ya, no shit. It isn't that easy though."

"Well, it should be a lot easier for you now. I will pull my men back, nobody from the family will touch another Nation member. You guys should be able to get to them with no problems."

"And how would you like this done?"

"I don't care how, just that it happens. It has to be done tonight though. You need to hit what's left of the top guys."

"And the others?"

"Cut the head off of the dog, the tail will stop wagging. We will take care of any stragglers who may try to rebuild."

"So, we do this, and the war stops?"

Yano nods, "And only if you do this, tonight."

Yano stands and turns as he walks away from Smith. Vinnie and Antonio follow, not one look back to see Smith's reaction.

That night was quite bloody. Twelve men left in the white brotherhood's top ranks, fourteen men found in various locations throughout the prison. Two Nation members fell victim in this massive surprise attack but the white boys are decimated, so all in all, not a bad loss. Smith had a personal grudge against the president of the brotherhood. He was found and beaten by Smith personally. He was found beaten to death, lying on the bathroom floor with burns all over his body. He was left lying with all of the showers turned to hot and the burning puddles they made rushed towards his limp body. He was beaten with a broomstick. After the beating, the stick was pushed about twelve inches up inside his anus. The guards were not sure if he died from the beating, the burns that covered sixty percent of his body, or the fact that he was turned into a vanilla popsicle.

After this night, the brotherhood was gone, and in only a few short months, as promised, Yano handled all stragglers that tried to rebuild and the family took one hundred percent control of the gambling ring on the inside. Yano and Marty ended up settling on ten percent of the Nation's drug trade, so money was coming in at Yano from a few different angles. Yano was not greedy, he pays his men accordingly. No problems are needed within the members of the family. After paying them and certain guards to look the other way, Yano did not see a big profit, well, not as big as he wanted to see. He quickly began to ponder taking full control of the drug ring. Is another war worth the reward? Does he have the power to defeat Marty or will he end up destroying what he has been building for so long now? Yano has plenty to think about before jumping to a decision.

Year four rolls around and Vinnie is being paroled. As he is about to leave he stops by to see Yano.

"You take it easy in here boss."

"I want you to head to my old neighborhood and look in on my mom for me. If you're planning on sticking around anyway."

"Well, I'm going to be looking for a way to make a living out there so I don't know where I'll end up."

"Why don't you go meet up with my brother, Gino. He knows about you, I have mentioned you and your importance to me in a few letters before. He will welcome you and help you find work."

"I appreciate that, Yano. Try not to get into trouble so you can get out soon."

"I have about six more years before I'm even eligible."

"Well, maybe, let me think of something."

Yano looks into Vinnie's eyes, he knows Vinnie will not let him down. He never has before. Though, Yano cannot even fathom any type of idea that he could come up with to get him released early, short of breaking him out that is. Yano smiles at Vinnie and wishes him well. As Vinnie turns to leave, Yano turns and heads back into his broom closet-sized bedroom.

Vinnie had no intention of heading back to Chicago. Omaha was his destination. As Vinnie walked to the bus station to buy a ticket, the cashier asked, "Where too?" Vinnie looks up with a smile and says, "Omaha, Nebraska".

As Vinnie pulled into town he began asking neighbors about the Scarpacci family. It didn't take Gino long before hearing of a strange man asking questions about him. This made him nervous, karma coming back to bite him in the ass? He immediately phoned Dino and Angelo. The two met up with Gino at his home, he did not want to leave his sisters alone before this stranger's identity was discovered and he was taken care of.

As Angelo sat at Gino's house with him, Dino headed down to the bus station. He drove around thinking that that would be the best place to find a new face in town. He finally notices a young unfamiliar face speaking with an elderly lady. Dino watches him trying to figure out who he could be. A lot of people have heard of Yano's murder conviction that happened just shortly after Don Talapini's death. When people tried to put two and two together, most of them got four. It wasn't hard to figure out. People know that after Yano and his the guys went on their rampage, the neighborhood turned around. So nobody was willing to turn on Gino and his family, especially to an outsider like Vinnie. Could he be a friend of some sort? Or maybe an enemy? A family member or close friend to one of the victims?

Dino parked across the street and watched Vinnie. He exits his vehicle and walks up to the building. Vinnie notices him and comes toward.

"Hey!"

Dino kept walking.

"Hey! Sir!"

Dino looks back over his left shoulder and sees Vinnie jogging towards him.

"You talking to me?"

"Yeah. Do you know the Scarpacci family?"

"Who wants to know?"

"I do".

"And who the fuck are you?"

"You must be Dino…"

Before he could finish, Dino snatches him by the shoulders and pushes him up against the building.

"And who the fuck are you?"

"Vinnie, my name's Vinnie Marino. I'm looking for Gino Scarpacci".

"What do you want with Gino and how do you know my name?"

Vinnie begins to mention Yano and Dino instantly dragged him into a nearby alley. As he pulls a pistol and puts the barrel to Vinnie's cheek he says,

"You're meddling in business you ought not to be meddling in, kid."

"Woah, Woah, Woah! Calm down. I'm friends with Yano".

Vinnie began his story and Dino put his pistol away. After he heard the explanation he took Vinnie to meet Gino.

"Sorry about the way I acted back there kid. New faces make us nervous. Especially when they come around asking for one of the guys who helped turn this neighborhood around."

Back At Gino's

T HE GUYS SIT at Gino's and listen intently to the stories Vinnie tells. He tells of the war, the gambling ring, and the drug fight. The gang cannot believe what Yano has done on the inside. As they talk amongst themselves, Vinnie jokes about the way in which he was greeted by Dino.

"Definitely not the hospitality that Yano told me to expect. More like walking back into prison."

"It was…" Gino began

"Until about three years ago," Angelo interrupts.

"The neighborhood was at peace for three years and then some guys starting causing trouble and we don't know who it is."

"What do you mean," Vinnie asks.

"Robberies, thefts, assaults and even a few murders," says Dino.

"They left a message painted on a wall once," Angelo started, "that for everybody who fights back, two Italians will pay the ultimate price."

Vinnie couldn't believe what he was hearing. Yano got a strong ten to twenty-year stretch for making the neighborhood safer and it only lasted three years.

"well, we can't let these fuckin' guys undo everything you guys did. All the risks you took, Yano's imprisonment, it'll all be for nothing if we don't stand up."

As Dino stands he mumbles, "that would be a death sentence for all of us and we don't have the weapons or manpower to hit as hard as we would need to. Plus we have no idea who we're hitting."

Back In The Prison

BACK IN THE prison, Yano was able to get to one of the guards. He began paying him for information on cell searches and anything that has to do with Smith. The guard was spying on Smith and trying to find out anything he could about the drug trade inside the walls. The guard comes back a few days later and tells Yano of a conversation he overheard about a shipment coming in from up north. A guy Smith called, 'Jonny Eyes', was the one bringing it in. He poses as a member of Smith's legal team so guards are not allowed in their visitation room. The switch fro money to drugs was quite easy.

As this day was approaching, and Jonny was set to arrive, the guard comes in and yells out, "Scarpacci! Visitor!" Smith is stunned, he should also be seeing Jonny though his name is never called. Yano was smiling as he walked into the room with Johnny Eyes. He was stealing Smith's product and connection right in front of his face and Smith is filled with anger. This is a very bold move on Yano's part. The confidential guard was able to get him the phone number that Smith was calling, and Yano was able to get it to Dino. From there Dino was able to figure out who's number it was from a woman in the neighborhood, who works as an operator, it took a few days but she found Johnny. Dino and Angelo went and visited him, pistols pulled and politely explained to Johnny that his days selling inside of the prison were now concluded. Johnny did not want this steady cash flow to end and made a deal agreeing to sell to them instead of Smiths boys. Angelo asks,

"wouldn't you rather be working with Italians anyways? Make money with your own people, not the coons."

"Shit man, I don't care. I go where the money is and colored folks love this shit, anything that will change their state of mind, from booze to pills. They'll take it all."

When Yano came back out of the room, folder, and briefcase in hand, Smith knew. It was he who had previously walked out of that room with those items. Smith knows what happened and he is ready for war. As Yano got back to a cell he opened the folder, it was one piece of paper that said, '$4500'. This is what he owed for the shipment he opened the briefcase and saw that it was full of prescription pain pills, about $20,000 worth. Smith is now frantically running to Yano's cell and is immediately stopped physically by Yano's henchman. Smith starts yelling, he is pissed, he is angry that the two men had the balls to put their hands on him. He began yelling at Yano, screaming of a war that they could never win. Yano stands, walks to his cell door, and looks up at Smith.

"You're done."

Simpler words were never spoken, then turned back and went back to what he was doing. He could almost feel the light turning green as he turned his back on Smith, who was, after all, one of the deadliest men in that prison for so long before. Though Yano knows this, he still sits with a smile. Unbothered.

Gino

GINO'S ALMOST 17 now and has begun to think about the future. It's been a couple of years since his brother went away and he feels like he's moving on from the old life. Gino originally wanted to be a lawyer, he remembered once when they were all still together Angelo said,

"Too bad one of us is in a lawyer, or a judge at least, because we if we get caught we're gonna need one on our side."

That always stuck in gino's head, so he started boosting trucks with Angelo to save money for law school. To Gino, this was a good idea. All he knew so far was a life of crime and to fund a life of law, though it may be corrupt law, crime seemed to be a perfect way.

Dino was making a few good connections, people to sell the pills too. Johnny Eyes would make a trip to town for a double delivery once a week. One package Gino would take to Dino, the other would go with Johnny to the prison for Yano. Dino paid for the first payment of $4,500 for Yano and he did it for two reasons. One, out of respect. Dino and Yano are really good friends, and Yano was a friend, who at the moment, Dino believes is in need. The second reason is to let Yano know that things are going well for them out there. He didn't want to tell him about the Italians creeping back in. He did not know who they were, nobody did. So to tell him about it would be to get his imagination acting up out of control for no reason. It would cause him to worry about the neighborhood, his brother, his mother, and his sister. This seems to be unwarranted to pass along this information. Dino does not want Yano to do something that could cost him his early release. Vinnie has been coming up with ideas to get Yano's early release bumped up even earlier.

Gino and Angelo have become quite the little two-man thieving crew. Trucks would come from all neighborhoods, but if any drove through Little Italy in Omaha, none of them left with the same contents in their truck. From dresses to suits, to kitchen equipment, the boys took it all. If a truck is worth loading that full of those goods then they must be worth money and the boys could sell it.

Gino can't help but wonder if the crime is even worth it anymore. Without his brother around and Don Talapini being dead, what's the point? The crime was never a way of life for them, it was never something they were born into, it was never something he was raised to be. It's something that they fell into with the murder of Enzo, their father. Gino's need for vengeance is no longer consuming his everyday life, maybe crime doesn't pay. He doesn't feel good about what he did in the past nor does he feel bad about it; he doesn't feel at all. Being a lawyer, and someday a judge sounds appeasing to him now. Will he ever be able to truly leave this life of crime or will there always be something appealing about the fast cash and the instant revenge that he is more than willing to do these days that will keep calling him back to that life?

Meanwhile

"THIS FUCKIN' GUY has only been here for four or five years, he thinks she's just gonna come in and take control of my business! He steals my Contact of sixteen fuckin' years and just completely cuts me out! Oh, he has another thing coming, he's gotta go! He's going to die and I'm doing this job myself! I'll get back in touch with Johnny, but in five years when I'm paroled, I'm killing him to that backstabbing piece of shit. I should have known those Italians stick together."

Smith complains to his cellmate, which happens to be his right-hand man, all night about Yano being a dead man already and that he just hasn't fallen yet. Smith was dumbfounded that Yano had the balls to pull such a move off. He never saw it coming, but he vowed to never let it go any further or leave it unpunished.

As the sun rose on another incarcerated morning, Antonio is awakened by the sound of clanging. Smith was dragging his metal cup back and forth across the bars of their cell door. Antonio rolls over and sees Smith.

"If you value your life, you won't be here at lunchtime."

Smith knows that Antonio and Yano are close. He knows that Antonio is in for murdering a man trying to help Gino. Smith also knows that that little message of his will not stray far from Yano's ear for long. Smith is hoping and betting on Antonio telling Yano. Of course, Antonio jumps out of bed and wakes Yano with the news.

"Something is happening at lunchtime. Smith is gunning for you."

Yano rolls over and sits up. As he rubs the sleep from his blue eyes he says that he is going to take a shower and then they will discuss what needs to be done. As Yano goes for a walk toward the shower, Smith is close behind. Smith and his goons enter only moments after Yano.

"You think you're a big man, don't you?"

"What?"

"You stole my supplier right out from under me! You destroyed my business!"

"Well," Yano starts, "Do you want a job?"

Yano was serious though Smith took this comment as an insult.

"No, I don't want no fuckin' job! I want my God damn shit back!"

"Hey, you can either take the job or shut the fuck up. Do you want to keep this up? We will end up going back to war, and it's a war that you won't win."

Yano knows that since the last war, Smith's numbers have increased exponentially more than the Italian numbers, though he stays strong and tries to bluff Smith.

"If we take this to war ten nobody makes any money. We then go on twenty-three hours per day lockdown or in the hole. You want that? It's nothing personal Smith. Its only business."

"Fuck your job!"

"I will even pay you fairly, hows thirty-five percent sound? See Smith, I'm not a greedy man. I'm just a businessman who knows how to get things done. I'm a much better businessman than you are.

Smith shakes his head at Yano. He doesn't want a war. He knows that there is power in numbers and he has the numbers. The way that

Yano spoke, Smith not being able to win the war, was a direct threat towards himself Smith thought. He settles for Yano's deal, for now, and his goons and he head back the way in which they came. Shortly after, Antonio meets up with Yano.

"What happened?"

"I'm not sure, but tell everyone to be on guard. I may have started another war."

A few days passes with no conflict with Smith, until the morning in which Yano's fifth year of incarceration began. Antonio is again awakened by an odd sound. There was no metal cup rubbing on cell door bars this time. It was the sound of a man grunting. Antonio looks over and sees Smith standing above Yano. His arm flailing up and down. A shiny blood-soaked object in his hand. A knife. As his arm came down, the blade pierces Yano's flesh. As it raises again, blood comes out with the blade, splattering on the wall and pooling on Yano's bed. He was stabbed twelve times in the stomach and right side before Antonio was able to understand what was happening and jump from his bunk to come to Yano's aide.

Antonio threw Smith to the floor and kicked him in the face. He turns to check on Yano and sees a hurt man, choking on his blood. Yano's lungs were filling and he was slowly suffocating. Antonio dramatically runs threw the hall yelling for the guards to come help. As he leaves Yano's side, another man by the name of Rocco enters. Rocco picks Smith up from the floor and drags him out of the cell. He then lifts Smith and tosses him over the banister. Smith's body falls four stories and lands headfirst upon the concrete floor. Rocco is able to leave unnoticed before the guards arrive and rush the two men to the infirmary.

Yano and Smith are treated in the infirmary but their wounds are too great for what little supplies the prison had. They were run to St.

Francis Cabrini Hospital, treated, and then put into a room marked critical condition. Neither was expected to survive the night.

Smith's wounds were almost all superficial. Scrapes and bruises from the fall, however, the head first landing had broken his neck as well as fractured his skull. The blood in the brain began to clot, no oxygen was able to get there, and soon it began to swell. After a few days, the swelling subsides and Smith is checked off the doctor's list. There is nothing more that they can do for him, other than send him to a facility that can care for brain dead patients. He will never again be able to move his body parts. Never again be able to taste his food, or smell the beautiful scent of a woman's perfume. Never again be able to even have a thought, or dream a dream of home. A life condemned to starring at whichever wall stands in front of him is all that he has left. Blank stares and dreamless nights.

A week passes before Yano finally wakes. Belly soar from the multiple penetrations of a foreign object. He tries to move but cannot. He opens his eyes to see that he is secured to the hospital bed. Though not in the prison hospital, he is still an inmate and a flight risk and must be treated as such. It will be a few more days until the doctors are ready to discharge him and send him back to prison, so the only thing he can do is relax. Take advantage of the big comfortable bed in which he now lies.

The Prodigal Boss Returns

WHEN YANO RETURNED to the Correctional Facility, he was expecting a war. He was expecting an act of revenge by the new boss almost as soon as he got there. He was more nervous today than he was when he first arrived 5 years ago. It's for sure now, someone wants him dead. As he walks into his cell, he notices nothing out of the ordinary. It's a peaceful quiet day and that makes him notice something. Smith, the leader of all that is said and done for every black male in this place, is pretty much dead. So why is it so peaceful? They should be going out of their minds he thought. Rocko stopped by his cell to see how he was feeling and filled him in on what he has missed.

"As soon as Smith's body dropped, and we got you some help, Antonio and I went to work. You weren't even out of the door yet and our soldiers were dropping them monkeys to their knees all over the prison. Only the top of the Zulu chain was hit, which means all of Smith's button men are still alive but no one to give them orders. We haven't even been hit back yet."

There's been no retaliation whatsoever. Maybe because they're afraid, maybe because they're afraid of not only what Yano is capable of but also willing to do. Maybe it's just because they're busy fighting amongst one another. Everyone wants that top seat, and they are killing each other for it. Or maybe it's just because they're done fighting altogether.

"So far no new leader has been announced."

"It's because they do not have any respect for themselves," Yano states. "Or for the business that they want to try and run. They have no orders, no structure. That type of behavior is how colored People are. They're savages. It's just in their genes to be violent, you would never see that happen with Italians."

The two sit and talk for a while And then Antonio showed up.

"Hey Yano, how you feeling? Has Rocco filled you in with everything ?"

Yano answers yes and says that he needs some rest. Rocco and Antonio sit outside of Yano's cell as guards and play some cards. No one is going to rise with any new conflicts at this moment, so everyone finally has a chance to relax, but all of these troubles Yano's thoughts. He can't help but think that some black man is going to kill him as proof of power, hoping to use it as leverage in becoming the new leader of the Zulu nation.

Yano was now a boss. As a boss, you have many more worries than a regular employee. As a boss, you are in charge of keeping the order. You are in charge of keeping people in line. He was almost twenty-five years old and already a boss, and this is the only subject that crossed Yano's mind

Some of his employees were in their forties and fifties, how can a twenty-five-year-old kid give orders and keep a man in line who is twice his age? What's to stop them from sneaking up and snapping his neck and taking the position for themselves? He thinks all night and the only thing that he could come up with was structure and respect. You have to have both qualities in every man. You have to have respect for yourself. You have to have respect for your friends, then you have a structure.

Only then will structure work, but a man who has no respect can bring the entire brigade down. So membership to this new organization was going to be exclusive. Yano needed to make some changes.

The warden of the facility has started hearing rumors about Yano's involvement in gambling, drugs, and almost three dozen murders. The warden was disgusted that his crew has been allowed to get away with it all for so long. He ordered confidential checks on all prison employees. He checked pay stubs to see how much the guards made. He then cross-checked their finances with how they lived to make sure everyone was living within their means. Needless to say, he was not pleased with allegations of corruption with his employees.

Frank Horn, that is the warden's name. Warden Horn found a man in his system who only averages eight thousand dollars per year and was seen driving to work in a twenty thousand dollar car. This caught the warden's attention, so he called the man in for questioning. It happened to be a guy named Morse. This was the same guy who retrieved all of the drug information from Smith's Phone calls for Yano.

When Morse was brought in for questioning he cracked almost immediately. This guy was singing before his ass ever even felt the hard plastic seat of his chair. Morse saw how the inmates lived and the things that they go through on a day-to-day basis. He did not want to end up like them, he did not want to end up with them. Ending up in the same spot as them would be bad news, he knew that he has mistreated many of the inmates and knew that if he ended up here he would not live for very long. He answered every question honestly that was asked of him, and even a few that weren't, he told on every other guard who was crooked. They were all fired for the suspicion but you can't charge someone with a crime based on suspicion and word of mouth, so no charges were ever filed against any of them.

The warden did have Yano's cell searched. He has been gone, in the hospital, so never had a chance to re-up on his dope stash. The guards found only a small bag containing approximately twenty pills that Antonio had forgotten about. When the warden approach Yano, he asked about them in which Yano replied,

"Warden, you know I've been gone for almost two weeks. If you wanted to catch me with something you should have searched me right after I left. Those pills are not mine. Smith probably dropped them during his crazy ass assault".

Warden Horn does not believe Yano, considering Smith attacked Yano while he was fresh out of bed, in his shorts with no clothes on. Where would Smith have kept the pills at? He offered Yano a deal,

"You have only five years until your first parole view review. This drug charge and one word for me, you will do the entire twenty years, no early release. Now with that being said, you can have your drug charge and another fifteen years, or you can go to the hole for an undisclosed amount of time and I will lose the pills. The parole board will know nothing about it, then when you come out of the hole and back into the general population, you will stay on your best behavior. When the time comes, I promise I will give my recommendation to the parole board. That means a guaranteed release date, it's a smart deal. It's a fair deal, you should take it".

Antonio stands up and is about to admit to the pills, but before he can get a full word out, Yano puts a hand on his shoulder. Antonio looks back at Yano, he sees the way his head nods towards him as if to say 'shut your mouth, I got this'. Yano is growing fond of running a criminal enterprise, but he wants to go where the real money. That's not in the prison, that would be outside of the prison walls. It didn't take Yano long to decide. He agrees that the pills were his and leaves with the warden and they lock Yano in his new cell. As the warden turned to walk away, he asked,

"So how much time down here are we talking about?"

The warden answers,

"As much time as it takes to separate your little crew."

"What do you mean separate? You just put me in a closet in the basement, how much more separate do you want us?"

The warden responds with one word.

"Transfers."

Paroled

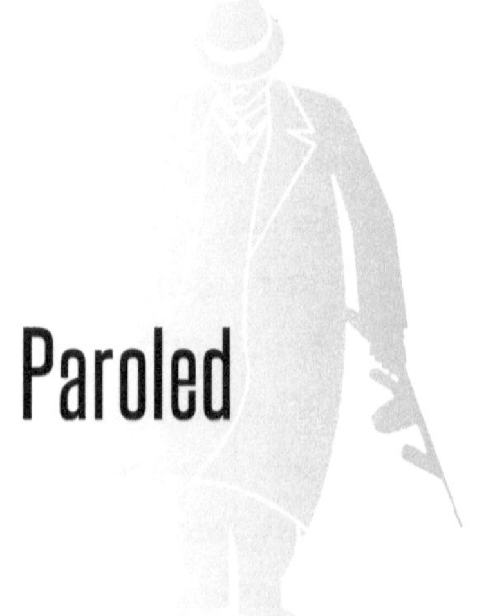

A COUPLE OF DAYS after Yano enters the hole he gets a note. The note is passed to him from an inmate who is handing out lunch trays. The note reads that Antonio is getting paroled and leaving the prison any minute. Yano asked the inmate if Antonio is still in the prison and the inmate says yes. Yano writes his note on a piece of paper and hands it back to the messenger.

"Get this to Antonio before he leaves."

The messenger finishes passing out his trays in quickly rushes back to Antonio.

The message was his address along with Gino's name as well as Morse's.

'There is a job to be done' it says, 'wait to hear from me.'

Knock knock knock, Gino jumps from his couch, Dino hides behind a door clutching onto a loaded shotgun. Gino slowly walks to the door, grabs the nob, turns the handle. As he's pulling the door open Dino cocks the shotgun and aims.

"Are you Gino?"

"Yes. Who the fuck are you?"

"The names Antonio Caruso. I just finished an eight-year stretch from killing that guy who killed your little Irish friend. Remember?"

Yeah, yeah, yeah, I remember you. What do you want with me?"

"Well the last six years of my sentence, I was with your brother. He gave me your address, told me that you and me gots a job to do."

"Another job? He just sent us another guy named Vinnie, who was also locked up with him? You know him?"

"Yeah, Vinnie Marino. Good guy, good guy."

"So what's the job?" Gino asked.

Antonio explains the job in the details in which Yano had given to him. Gino doesn't understand why he needs his help.

"Why does Yano want me to do this?"

"Explosives. He told me that your friend Patty, that was killed, taught you how to make car bombs."

"Yeah, that's right, but it's been a long time."

"Can you still make them?"

"Well, of course, I can still make them. I even made improvements. I've made a few over the years."

"So, what's the problem?"

"Well, the problem is that I made a few, but I have used none of 'em. I'm not sure if they work the way I make them.

"Well, how do you make them? What are the mechanics?"

"Well I make a stick of dynamite, Then I put a piece of flint at the top. Attached to that I have a piece of steel with a long rope wrapped around it. I tie one side of the bomb to the front axle and I tie the back part of the rope to the back axle. As the car begins to drive, the axle pulls the rope which pulls the flint against the steel, causing a spark, lighting the gunpowder, then boom no more driver."

"Are you sure will kill him?"

"Hell fuckin' yeah I'm sure"

"How?"

"Because I put the explosive side under the front axle, it explodes right underneath the driver seat, but it doesn't matter if I put the bomb in the back because then it explodes the gas tank and the car blows up even bigger."

"Well, theoretically it sounds good."

"Your got damn right it sounds good. I'm not a fuckin' idiot. If there's one thing I learned from my big brother it's to plan things out. After you plan 'em out, plan them out again. After you plan them out again, double check your first plan and make sure it works with the second plan, and then come up with your final plan. That mother fucker ain't stupid either, he taught me to do things right or don't do them at all."

The Plan In Action

MORSE IS LEAVING a shopping center one day, both arms full of groceries. His vision is blocked by sacks of food. He does not see Gino frantically jump from the Bushes, run across the parking lot, slide under his car, and hook up a bomb. He does not notice Gino barely getting away before he, himself, reaches his car again. It has been a while since Gino has killed anyone, he was nervous. As Gino ran away Morse sat his groceries down and was searching for his keys. Gino made a mistake. The rope tied to the back axel slipped and the bomb dropped. The type of car bomb Gino had rigged up was supposed to explode when the car drove away, but it did not. The bomb fell and tugged the thin nylon rope just right. The flint pulled out, not all the way, just enough to rub along the steel and light a spark.

As Morse exposed the keys from his pocket the car explodes, his body is lifted and thrown across the pavement ripping his blistered skin and breaking a few bones. He did not die, though if the bomb would have detonated on time or even a few seconds late it would have trapped him in the car and he would have burned him alive. Gino knew that Morse is not going to die but he also feels that Yano will accept this as Morse's punishment. His skin is melted, the flash from the bomb was bright enough to blind Morse permanently and create a disfigured look as his skin would never heal the same.

Antonio does not see it that way. He runs over to Morse's limp burnt body and hits him in the head with a pipe. He found one on the ground, swung his arm upward, and slammed it back down. He hit him square on the back of the head once. After that, a cop had come running out of the store and tackled him. Antonio was charged with the entire assault and, after being a free man for only a few short weeks, was sent back to jail for another five years. If Morse had died from the pipe hit Antonio would have received a lot longer sentence.

Paramedics lifted Morse on to the Gurney and up into the back of the ambulance. He already knew. He knew what happened and he knew why it happened. He didn't have to contemplate it. Actions in his past were the reason this happened to him and he knew it. He might not have known that it was Yano, but he knew that it was either the Italians or the Blacks in the prison system. He knew that somebody was after him. It could have even been a guard that he snitched on. His face was melting from his skull because he was a rat, but did the guards have the capability and the know-how to plant a car bomb? That seems more like a gangster hit then a revenge hit from upset fellow employees.

The news of Morse's hit makes its way back to Yano. He is upset but not mad. He wanted Morse dead for betraying everybody. Yano also understands that sometimes, some things are far worse than death, and the way that Morse has to live now is a far worse punishment than death. Living a disfigured life and constantly being reminded by it every time he looks in the mirror is far worse than just dying. Dying is too easy for Morse, his punishment must be much harsher.

Twelve months go by and Yano is finally released from the hole. As he walks out and into the sunlight he feels the pain in his eyes from sitting in the dark for so long. Yano feels as if the sun has gotten closer to the earth 'cause it never used to seem this bright before. As he goes to his cell he stops at Antonio and smacks him hard on the cheek.

"You ruined my plans by getting me sent down there, and then you ruined them even more by getting your fuckin' ass sent back here. I wanted you out there with my brother, Angelo, Vinnie, and Dino to start getting some money collected for the future. Big plans are being put into action."

He plans to keep his neighborhood clean happy and loyal to one another. He plans to always keep extortionists like the Black Hand out of the neighborhood. He does not know that the organization is moving back in. He does not need to know about what would need to happen to remove this insane tumor from his neighborhood. Yano turns to Antonio and tells him to keep everything running on the right track, but to leave him out of it all. He told him to have a trusted friend bring down all his money and any messages. Yano needs to appear as if he quit running the organization so he can get an early release.

"Do you really trust with the warden says?" asks Antonio.

"I don't have a reason not to besides, if he fucks me over he'll have another ten years to deal with me. If he thinks the crime rate is bad in here now, wait until the parole board denies me."

Antonio knows Yano is getting very angry because of the language that he is using. Yano usually speaks as if he was very educated, so he just agrees and lets Yano walk away.

As Gino sits at Angelo's house, he gets a phone call from Rosaria. She is scared, she says that two big Italian guys are knocking on their door. Gino hurries home and calls Dino and has him meet him and Angelo at his mother's house. As they all arrived at Fina's house, the men gone. They walk up to the house and notice that the door has been kicked in, windows were broken, and all of Fina's religious figurines have been smashed. Rosaria was on the floor crying, they broke in and started ripping the house apart. Yano isn't going to like this.

Year Eight

A S YEAR EIGHT rolls around of Yano's sentence, a new man arrives in prison, Frances "Frankie" Ruggerio. Antonio approaches him and talks with him. He seems like a good guy and Antonio takes him to meet Yano.

"When you meet Yano, be respectful. Do not call him by his name. He is to be called Sir, or boss, but you don't say boss yet because you're not in the business. Do not speak until he speaks to you, do not ever question any of his orders, and never approach him alone until your trust is fully gained. Oh and another, thing I know we're in prison but watch your fuckin' mouth when you speak to him, that takes us back to being respectful. Yano sees swearing as a sign of weakness, says by acting like anything less than a gentleman to your superiors shows a complete lack of respect and if you disrespect him then you're done."

"What do you mean I'm done? And how will I know when I'm completely trusted?"

"That means you'll be put out of business, and an Italian that does not run with the rest of the Italians runs with no one. Being alone in prison is worse than being dead. Besides, if you're alone the niggers will kill you off within a month. That's after they use you as their bitch for a few weeks. It won't be just one man either, every black man in this joint will have a turn or two. As for the trust thing, well, in this business you can't ever really completely trust anyone, but when you're in good enough, someone will let you know."

Out on the yard, the Zulu Nation is having a meeting. There are about fifteen men were standing around, no one trusting anyone. Every one of their eyes moving back and forth, watching everyone else. There are about four hundred angry, nervous, dangerous, black men in the prison; all wanting that top dog seat. Finally, the man who organized the meeting spoke.

"My name is James. Now, most of you here already know me and the ones who know me well know me by the name Jaybird, but for those of you who don't I'm the cousin of Marty Smith. I called this gathering today because we need to figure out what the fuck we're doing. Every day that we're fighting amongst each other, we lose money. Those God dam daigo wop mother fuckers are sitting back there laughing at us, and I for one am sick and tired of having to look over my shoulder for one of them greaseballs to run up on me and over my other shoulder for those cock eating white boys. All the while I'm also wondering which one of my People might try and bump me off and it's bull shit. We need a leader. I called you specific fourteen men here because I've noticed that we, out of every other brother locked up here are the worst. Fuck everyone else, everyone here is going to be a someone in our new regime. We need to just figure out who will be the boss and right-hand man, everyone else will be shot callers and run your crews according to the boss' rules. You also pay dues every month, drug use will be forbidden, that's how people slip up. Junkies are untrustworthy. They're useless, the penalty for that will be death, junkies get caught up and snitch. We cannot have that or this thing will not work."

Everyone at the meeting is happy with this new arrangement. It's like they're all a boss who all just happened to have another boss above them.

"If you notice one of your men using you will not kill them yourselves without first coming and discussing it with the big boss. All decisions go through that one man and no one else."

Another man yells out, "I thought the penalty was death! You just said that now you're saying not to kill him? I don't understand."

James replies, "Yes, the penalty will be death, eventually, but the boss needs to know about it first for two reasons. Number one, anyone can kill a man for any reason and think he is justified just by calling him a doper after his departure. We need to know so we can check him out and make sure the call for his death is legit. Second of all, we might be able to use that man, or men, as fall boys. If we're having problems with the guineas or the crackers, we can use the fall boys to settle it. That way if they lose and get killed, well fuck it. They were dead men walking anyway; by some chance, they complete their jobs then we'll take them out afterward. This way we're not losing our good, trustworthy, loyal, strong-hearted men. Breaking any rules will also mean death unless the actions are so powerful that they can be justified, but again, that will be the big boss' decision.

Another man by the name of Rafael Lee steps up.

"I think it's only right for Marty Smith's cousin, James, to be boss. Marty started this click and I think that is how he would have wanted it, and Marty was a good friend of mine as he was to most of you."

Everyone else agrees, all happy just to be getting a top seat at the table with a little power. They were all tired of being somebody else's button man.

"You're kind of trying to run the business like an Italian would, what's up with that?"

"I know that we all hate the Italians and you should, we should, but you have to respect them. They know how to run a loyal, respectful, business and without loyalty, there is no order; without order, there is no business. So yeah, we are going to organize like the Italians, but not because we want to be like them it's because of how they do things works."

As the bells ring ou,t signaling chow time, Jaybird says one more thing,

"The first one to kill a top dog Italian will be my number one, my right-hand man."

They all turned away with a smile. It is a challenge that they're all up to accept.

The Return of The Hand

"HOLY SHIT GUYS," Gino starts. "I just saw a couple of guys that I haven't seen in the neighborhood for years. They were Don Talapini's men."

The guys looked at Gino like he was crazy.

"That's who's coming back to the neighborhood, it's the old organization rebuilding, and that must have been who went to my mom's house. It's no secret that Yano was involved in their previous takedown. I don't know who's in charge or who's running shit now, but I swear to God the faces that I saw down the street were extremely familiar from the old days."

"What do you think we should do, Dino?" Angelo says.

"How the fuck do I know? The neighborhood's going to shit real fast, we can't just wait for Yano to come home, that's for sure."

"You're right. Angelo, we need to do something now."

"Yeah, yeah, I know. I also know that if we wait for Yano to come home, the neighborhood will be too far gone to even save again. We need to come up with a bunch of money and a bunch of guns, we can't fight these guys with baseball bats. We need to re-up our arsenal like we used to have."

Dino stands and begins to talk to the boys. He speaks of how they are speaking bull shit. Yano isn't guaranteed to come home anytime soon, and they need to get their heads out of their asses.

"Yano still has twelve years left if he doesn't get paroled, and parole is never a guarantee." He turns and spits on the ground, "It's horrible to even speak that way but his chances of being released in two years are slim to none. We need to act now. Gino, you and Angelo are going to need to start boosting more trucks. We need a lot of money and fast."

"Trucks have changed their roots though Dino. They haven't been coming through here in months, and we don't even know anybody who will buy the shit anymore. We got too hot from all the previous heists."

"You let me worry about that. Listen, we'll boost trucks in the black, Irish, and Polish neighborhoods. Then we'll sell the goods to the shops around here for half the price they are paying now. Cutting out the middleman will help everyone. Think about it, who cares if we sell the shit for half price, or even less. It's all profit for us, plus the shop owners will make more money so they can pay their dues to these fuckin' bullies that are taxing everybody, and still be able to put food in their family's mouths. It will make everyone happy, we're all making money."

"So, while we're out there boosting trucks and selling stolen goods what are you and Vinnie going to be doing?"

"Well, we'll do what Vinnie knows best, jewels. Just try not to get in trouble for it again, we need all the help we can get right now. I don't know your background but Yano wouldn't have sent you to meet his brother if he didn't trust you, not like that hot head Antonio. We sure could use his dumbass right now."

Later that night Dino and the other boys went about six miles down the road to a truck stop in a black neighborhood. Dino had Vinnie waiting in the car with the engine running in case they needed to make a quick getaway. Gino jumps in the driver's seat and pulls out two screwdrivers. He jabs one into the ignition and hands the other one to Angelo. Angelo runs off and hops into another truck and does the same. The two boys wiggle their screwdrivers back and forth, up and down, in and out, until finally, the trucks start. Dino runs back and jumps in the car with Vinnie and they take off. The boys follow in the big trucks, waiting a few minutes to turn on the headlights so nobody sees.

Angelo couldn't help but feel an extreme rush of excitement as he hit the headlights and took off. Dino drives in front to direct the boys back to the neighborhood. They stopped and parked their trucks in an empty field about a mile and a half from Dino's building. They didn't want the wrong people, or any people for that matter, to notice them unloading the goods. They quickly popped the lock on the backs of the trucks and started unloading boxes of unknown goods. The boys could only fit a few boxes and dino's car at a time. So Dino pointed to a little rundown shack a few blocks away. Gino and Angelo were to wait there so they could fit a few boxes more in the car. Every time Dino would leave, the boys would run back to the shack, and when Dino returned, so did the boys. This was a precaution in case the police drove by, the boys did not get caught at the scene.

Dino and Vinnie drove cautiously back to dino's grocery store and they unloaded the goods down in the basement. On the way back to the trucks, they continued the sequence of events until both trucks were empty. Dino's basement was full of boxes of unknown items. The only thing that was known for sure is that these items were worth money and Dino's basement was full.

While back at the store they started opening some of the boxes. The entire load from the first truck was all clothes and shoes, the second was all liquor. Dino was happy knowing they picked the right trucks and this kind of merchandise should be very easy to move. The next day the boys split up and all went to the different clothing, liquor, and shoe stores making their propositions directly to the owners. No other store employees were to know anything about this. They all made their deals and told them to cancel their business with original suppliers. If the black hand saw them getting twice the deliveries, eventually they're going to get suspicious. All of the stores paid cash upfront, and the merchandise was delivered later that day.

After all the money was collected, it tallied a little over twenty-five hundred dollars. The boys couldn't believe it. Dino was not satisfied however, he was angry that they had to leave half a truck of liquor behind. It was also disappointing that they could only make one trip a month because the stores couldn't sell the items fast enough.

"This isn't going to work," Dino mumbles. "We need to expand. I know of a decent-sized warehouse we could rent. It would easily fit five or six truckloads inside."

Vinnie replies, "We can't move that much at a time though, so what's it matter?"

"We can if we expand as I said. We can boost two trucks from each of the Polish neighborhood, the Irish neighborhood, and the black neighborhoods. We'll have to get shops in those areas to also buy from us. Who doesn't love to make more money so it shouldn't be an impossible task. We just have to keep the storehouse organized and never sell the stuff to the same neighborhoods from which we stole it. This way it'll lower chances of people noticing us."

Gino says, "Yeah, that could work, that could work. We'll boost two trucks per night, three nights a month. That should do it, except for the alcohol. We might need to hit four or five of those trucks per month. Then, we could also get a big ass safe or a vault or something to keep all the cash and the jewels when you and Vinnie startup that operation. The trucks actually might be big enough, jewels are a lot riskier and harder to move. I can just help out with the trucks."

Dino adds, "Jewels are more risk, yes, but diamonds move fast. I know a guy who can move them all. You and I will stick with that one or two jobs every few months should be fine. Those little shiny rocks are easy to move but not as easy to come by. They're not cheap material either like pants and shirts, people will shoot you for these."

Round One

I T HAS BEEN close to a month since Jaybird has taken control of the black criminal community inside of the prison. The order in his crew has been restored and peace has broken out. Everything was finally starting to calm down. Even the guards were starting to relax again. They were on edge from Morse's testimony, most corrupt guards were fired on suspicion. Others were left unpunished. However, Morse's 'accident' left some bad blood in the mouths of his few friends that he had left. The guards that still liked him and the many that didn't all knew that Yano had reached his long arm far beyond the concrete walls and touched him.

Concrete and stone could not keep his touch away from Morse. The cracked foundation and the miles of land in between the two men may as well be a few feet, Yano wanted him hit, and he was hit.

Jaybird and his men were not as worried, though impressed, he didn't care. He knew that Yano was resourceful, so he was not surprised. This outside incident was not going to ruin his inside plans. The greenlight to hit Yano's top men has been turned on. Everybody was beginning to relax, but the Nation was ready to pop off again.

Yano stood in front of Frankie. With Antonio and Rocko on either side, he tells how pleased he is.

"Nobody in this place has earned my trust and my respect as fast as you have, Frankie. You have been a loyal employee and a great enforcer. You never question my orders and you always follow them. For this reason, I am welcoming you to my crew. What we call, the family, will be just that, your family. We come before anything and anyone else."

With only the flickering light from a small candle, Yano reaches back and grabs a metal shard.

"I want you to know that from this day forth, I will not hesitate to bleed for you. Will you bleed for us?"

Frankie nods and responds with only one word, "Yes".

"Hold out your hand."

Frankie puts his hand out in front of him. Yano grabs hold of his four fingers and slides the metal shard across his palm. As his skin opens, blood pools in his hand and on to the floor.

"I want you to look at the blood exiting your flesh. This is symbolic of my blood on your hands. This shall be the only time it ever happens. You are to give your life for me if need be, as I will for you. Now, I want you to look at the blood on the floor. This blood pool is symbolic of your death if you ever betray us."

Yano speaks of loyalty and trust a while longer before entering Frankie to a high standing position in the family.

"You are now, what I like to call, a man of honor. You belong to me now, and nobody is allowed to touch you. Any insult towards you will be taken as an insult towards all of us."

As Yano welcomes Frankie to the family a scream is heard, "DIE!" The attention of all four men was captured immediately. A black man trying to earn the right hand of Jaybird is lunging at Yano. He swings his blade rapidly, willing to take out any of the three men but hoping to get the Italian boss. Any other man can kill every single one of Yano's top men but it would not add up to killing Yano himself he figured.

His blade finds his way to Antonio, slashing his across his face and cutting deep into his cheek. Rocko grabs the man and tries to push him back but the man was too strong. His blade finds its way to Rocko's stomach, cutting him deep but not fatally. Rocko falls. As he makes one last attempt at Yano, the two men stand back up, but not quickly enough. Frankie jumps in front of Yano and the cold, steel finds a home inside of his gut. The jagged shard rips an unfixable wound into Frankie's stomach and pierces his lung.

As Frankie falls he knocks Yano down. The man lifts his arm but before he can bring it back down, Antonio and Rocko are both beating on him. The man's jaw was almost instantaneously broken as Rocko lands his first punch. He falls to the floor and Antonio stomps on his head. His head bouncing between Antonio's foot and the concrete floor As Rocko's foot found room to sink into his ribcage. As the beating became more severe, Yano was able to climb out from under Frankie's limp body. Eyes watery, he held Frankie as he took his last breaths. He tried to speak to Yano but his lung was filling with blood and he was drowning. Blood spilled from his lips as he tried to utter a few last words. Within seconds his body lay lifeless and Yano yells at the two to stop the beating.

With Yano's parole hearing approaching, he could not be implicated in any further criminal enterprise, especially murder. He orders the two men to drag him someplace secluded and Yano walks away. Rocko runs and opens a nearby closet door as Antonio drags the man's broken body.

Yano walked to a group of Italians and instructed them to go outside and start a riot.

"You will probably be thrown in the hole for a week or two, but I need this to be done. For the good of the family, do not let me down. I need this place to be empty of all guards, so make this riot big and last as long as possible."

Yano walked back and gave one last look at Frankie laying in a pool of his blood, wiped the tears from his face, and enters the closet. The closet had multiple items that could be used as a weapon. The bloody man, sitting in a chair, looks up at Yano as best he could with his hurt neck. He says nothing, just stares. Yano stares back, also, no words spoke. In the background, an alarm can be heard. This is an indication that the riot has begun. Yano waits a few more minutes to make sure that all of the guards have left the area and then proceeds to go to work.

"You deserve to die very slow and painfully. Frankie, the man that you just murdered was a very dear friend of mine. These two men here, you also wounded. They are my most trusted and loyal men. You didn't even scratch me, yet I am hurt. Frankie was a true soldier, unlike you dumb fucking niggers. You think you can sneak up from behind us and that makes you a gangster? In my book, that makes you a pussy. You look a man in the eyes when you kill him. Frankie was untouchable, yet you touched him. Now, what are we going to do to make things right?"

Yano tells his men to each hold an arm as he walks behind him. He pulls an object from his pocket, something borrowed from the kitchen, a potato peeler. He then gently rests it upon the black flesh of the man's face and slides it down toward his chin slowly. Flesh peels, screams screamed, blood falls. After he slides it down each cheek he finds his way to the bridge of the man's nose.

As the peeler peeled, the alarms silenced. The rioters were being taken to the hole and the guards returning to their posts. Lockdown was initiated. Yano, Antonio, and Rocko leave the closet, but not before Yano sticks the peeler into the man's jugular. They all walk out and head back to their cells. The guards begin to fill the scene and Yano tells the guys to rid themselves of all bloody clothes and hit the showers.

The guards weren't back to their posts for ten minutes and the alarms began to ring again. Frankie's body had been found. Every inmate was locked in their cell as the investigation began. An Italian man lying dead in what seemed to be an ocean of blood left only one suspect, the Zulu Nation. There are hundreds of them and it would be impossible to tell who killed this man so as the leader, Jaybird was taken into custody for questioning.

It took three more days before the foul odor of Frankie's killer was noticed. A guard walking past the closet finally smelled it and went in to check. The smell instantly tripled once the door was opened and the guard immediately began to vomit. The smell of a dead man sitting in the heat for three days is not pleasant. The smell of the blood and the bugs that began to swim in it festered throughout the ventilation system and could be smelled in nearby cells. Maggots were beginning to live off of the pieces of the face that were peeled off and thrown into a trashcan as casually as a crumbled piece of paper.

The local police were brought in to assist in this investigation. Warden Horn and the police arrived at the scene with masks sprayed with perfume to hide the stench. Due to the severity of this homicide, the police wanted the warden to hand out death penalties to anyone found to be involved.

Rocko had been keeping an eye on the closet for three days waiting for the corpse to make its debut and finally, it has. He ran and told Yano that the body had been discovered. Yano gives Antonio a nod and Antonio quickly rushes out. The Warden and the police are beginning another lockdown and conducting cell searches for any evidence. Antonio was able to sneak into Jaybird's jail cell as he was still in custody and hide the bloody potato peeler in his locker. He also hid some of their bloody clothes in with his laundry. He was lucky enough to leave the cell just moments before the Warden had Jaybird's cell searched.

Jaybird's cellmate was a kitchen worker so he had easy access to any sharp weapons. Jaybird tries to explain to the Warden that his cellmate was sick and has been in the infirmary all week.

"This is bullshit!" he yells out.

The more he fought to prove his innocence the guiltier he appeared; as if he were hiding something.

"Why the fuck would I kill my man Warden?"

"You tell me."

"An Italian man was found dead the other day, this is, obviously, an act of revenge."

As the two argued, the police open Jaybird's locker and find the murder weapon. A deeper search turned up the bloody clothes. Jaybird cries about how Yano set him up. The Warden begins to believe him. Why would Jaybird be stupid and keep his bloody clothes? Why would he stash the potato peeler in his locker, getting blood all over more items? The Warden thinks; Yano hasn't been in trouble or even had one complaint against him for over a year since the two made their deal. He also knows of the tension that has been growing more and more between the blacks and Italians ever since Yano first arrived eight and a half years ago. The Warden and both white cops were racist against both blacks and Italians so they were happy with them killing each other off. No real investigation went any further, but Jaybird was going to be punished for having the contraband. The Warden took him down to the lowest level of the prison where they could all be alone.

"James Smith, you are hereby charged and found guilty of the severe, brutal, murder of one Charles Carry and Francis Ruggerio. You will be sentenced to death by firing squad. Do you have any last words?"

"You have got to be fuckin' kiddi…"

Jaybird never had the chance to finish his sentence before the three men pulled their pistols and fired multiple times each. Jaybird caught seventeen bullets to the head and chest and fell to the floor. Some would say that many shots are excessive but none would say it to the shooters. Jaybird was black and the shooters were white, that's all that mattered. This is the world that they are living in and they had to deal with it. There isn't a judge in the state that would convict these shooters. Anybody not white was viewed as less than human, less than a dog even. Blacks and Italians had no rightful place in this country except at the bottom of the river or locked away in some prison. That's exactly what happened to Jaybird. He was locked up for over ten years and then tossed in the river behind the facility. He probably even ended up being the butt of a few jokes after work hours and other white men would just laugh.

Yano is upset by what happened to Jaybird and feels real sorrow for his family. Yano did want him dead, but not like this. Yano only let it upset him for a couple of minutes. He then walked up to the black men sitting in the chow hall.

"Do any of you have a problem with what I did? If so, act on it right now."

Nobody said anything and nobody made a move. Even though the Nation was pissed, they understood it was all business and nothing personal. They understood that Frankie died in vain. They also understood that a revenge hit was inevitable. They knew that Yano wanted Jaybird gone just as much as he wanted Yano gone. One of them was bound to die. The man that killed Frankie, Charles, was a dead man walking for going after Yano. The Nation knew that that was an idiotic move. However, the way he was put down was savage. It was ridiculously unnecessary but inevitable.

"Jimmy says that he was setup. He says that he was set up by you, Yano. I almost believed him."

The Warden speaks and Yano knows that the Warden knows he isn't innocent in this.

"Ever since you got out the hole you have kept your ass out of trouble. So I chose not to believe that you were behind this. Well, it's all over now so you take your ass back to behaving for me or else. Don't think for a second I won't take that deal off of the table if you fuck around any."

Yano doesn't say a word as the Warden speaks. He simply nods and walks away after the Warden does.

The Robbery

DINO AND VINNIE drive about an hour and a half away from their neighborhood and arrive in a Polish area. This neighborhood is heavily populated but the Blackhand organization has never been able to get a foot in this particular door. The neighborhood is left unprotected and unwatched. This is a neighborhood where people mind their own business, keep to themselves, and handle their problems without calling the law.

The two pull up and park in front of a jewelry store and Vinnie walks in. Instantly, the two women working walk up to Vinnie, he explains that he is not looking to buy quite yet. He is just getting prices on diamond earrings for his girlfriend. As Vinnie walks around he is casing the place for a job. There are thousands of dollars worth of jewels in this place. He looks up and notices a room in the back.

"May I use your bathroom," he asks.

The woman nods and points down the hallway. Vinnie walks back and casually looks into the room, it is an office. As Vinnie stands in the bathroom he turns on the sink to avoid suspicion and uses the mirror to see across the hall into this office space. He notices a shotgun leaning up against the desk.

"I could grab the shotgun and rob them right now," he mumbles to himself.

"Then I'd end up back in the joint."

After reaching his senses he exited the bathroom. Walking back down the hall he glances in one last time and sees something, a safe.

Upon returning to the car he fills Dino in on the facts.

"I saw a safe in the wall, let's go get some tools and come get it."

"We don't need tools. We can just walk in, break it out of the wall, and take it back to the warehouse and open it."

"No, Dino. I am not going inside the store. We can take the safe from the outside, I saw where it is at."

"We're going in and taking the safe plus everything else!"

Dino begins to get annoyed.

"Why only steal half the goods? Why only get half of a payday?"

"Dino, you're getting greedy. This is why I went to prison in the first place. This is one hundred percent profit. We don't need to get everything. I'm not going back to jail for this."

Dino is upset but sees the reasoning, he is becoming greedy. The two leave and return about an hour later with some tools and a cart with wheels. As they entered the alley they continuously watched both ends for cars. The high buildings had a potential for witnesses as well. Too many factors to think of and too many places someone could witness something from.

The two take turns hammering the wall and watching for cops. Vinnie finally, after an hour of hammering, gets the safe to fall into the alley. As the two loaded it up on the cart, they heard a noise. It was the sound of that shotgun being loaded. They remembered watching the two cashier women leave but did not think to look in and see if the store manager or owner was in there. They quickly turn to run, pushing the cart as a shotgun blast rang out. Dino cringes but continues to run while Vinnie falls. Dino, unknowingly, ran to the car alone. As he went to lift the safe, he looked back and saw Vinnie lying in the alley, bleeding. Dino freaked out. He thought Vinnie had been killed, but without going to check on him or offering help of any kind, he loaded the safe and sped off. Vinnie was left for dead in a puddle of his blood.

As Dino's tires squeal out of their parking space, Vinnie stands. He is wounded in the leg. The shot grazed him but, still he walks with a severe limp. As the store manager barrels through the back door, shotgun still in hand, he sees Vinnie hobbling down the alley. He leans up against a small fence to rest and just as the man took aim again, Vinnie flips over the fence. He falls int the grass of a neighbor's yard. He manages to pull himself back to his feet and limp away. He only makes it a few blocks, staying in the shadows so as not to be seen before he collapses. He is found by an elderly woman. She is the one who reports the wounded stranger and gets him taken to the hospital.

Vinnie awakens from surgery and sees police officers as well as the doctor.

"We need you to tell us what happened son."

"I was robbed."

"Robbed? You were?"

"Yes. A black man robbed me. I turned to run away and he shot me."

The police were inclined to believe this story as he was found in the black neighborhood. Though reports of a gunshot had only come from the Polish area.

"You're sure that you were the one robbed?"

"Yes, sir."

The doctor chimed in with remarks about how Vinnie must have had a lot of adrenaline pumping through him. He should not have been able to run at all. The shot that appeared to be a graze at first actually blew out his knee. The knee cap had been shattered into so many pieces that the doctor was unable to repair it. The doctor says that it is his opinion that Vinnie will never be able to walk without the limp again. All of Vinnie's thoughts then shifted from the fear of heading back to prison if his true story had been found out, to the memory of Dino's face as he jumped in the car and left him for dead. His fear quickly changed to anger. Had Dino's ideals also shifted? Was he even in this to raise money to fight off the Hand anymore? Vinnie swore that he would kill Dino but had to get word to Yano first. This is one of Yano's most trusted friends, but Yano has been gone for a long time, and people change.

Dino returns to the warehouse, alone and nervous.

"Where is Vinnie?" Gino asked repeatedly.

"Dino! Where is Vinnie?"

"He's dead! Everything was going fine one minute, then the next he was dead. There was nothing I could do. We were loading the safe into the back of the car and the owner of the store noticed us. He came outside shotgun in hand and shot Vinnie twice. Or maybe three times, I don't fuckin know it happened fast and I didn't count the shots."

"Are you sure he's dead?" Angelo asked."Yeah, I saw his body. His head was blown apart. He's gone. I didn't have a choice but to leave him. I would've died too. I'm broken up about it guys, but really, there was nothing I could've done."

Gino and Angelo both turn to leave, heartbroken. Dino looks up and yells out,

"Don't you want to see what's in the safe?"

He lets out a little giggle and finishes.

"First we have to figure out how to get her open."

Gino and Angelo both look at each other. How could Dino be laughing, about anything, right now? By the tone of his voice, the two begin to figure that something doesn't add up. Gino leaves to write to Yano. Angelo stays he can't help but begin to wonder if Dino had Vinnie killed. Or if any of his stories are even true. Maybe Dino killed him himself.

Truths

THE FOLLOWING MORNING arrives and Gino wakes. He sits in his bed, looks out of the window, and listens to the bird's chirp. It seems as if a good day is about to start, but then the telephone rings.

"Gino!" his mother yells.

Gino walks downstairs and grabs the phone.

"Hello?" he asks.

It's Vinnie. Gin was in complete shock. Dino specifically said that he saw Vinnie's head blown up, he lied, but why? The two spoke long enough for Gino to get the true story, about how he was only hit in the leg once and shattered his knee cap. About how Dino got scared or greedy or whatever it was that caused him to leave Vinnie lying there to be caught or killed.

"Don't trust him, Gino. He is getting greedy and I think he is stealing from us. This isn't about freeing Yano for him anymore. It's all about making money, more money than the rest of us."

"I'm going to talk to Angelo and then Ill go see Yano I can't do anything until I speak with him. I'll swing by the hospital on my way home and visit you. Don't contact anyone else until I get there. I want

Dino to think that we're ignorant of the situation still. If he knows that we know the truth, well, there's no telling what hell do."

Gino heads to the prison for a sit down with his brother.

"How you doing big brother?" Gino asks as he hugs Yano.

"What brings you here?"

"Bad news."

Yano shakes his head as if to say, now what?

"Vinnie got himself shot. Well, I should say, Dino, got Vinnie shot."

Yano looks back up at his brother perplexed.

"What are you trying to say, Gino?"

"The two of them were out on a job and Vinnie got shot.'

"And this is Dino's fault, how?"

"I'm not exactly sure about that Yano. I just know that Dino cannot be trusted. Vinnie says he got shot running to the car, but Dino says that they were already by the car."

"Ok. Stories never match one hundred percent, Gino. That doesn't mean anything other than Vinnie knows that he fell a few steps sooner than when Dino noticed."

"Yeah, but it's more than that. Dino came back and said that Vinnie got hit two or three times but he only got hit once. Dino says that he looked back and saw Vinnie's head blown up but he only got shot in the leg. Dino bitched out and left him there that's the point, I'm, trying to make. He didn't even help and then he lied to make himself look innocent."

"That doesn't make any sense though. Why would Dino say that Vinnie was dead if he didn't think that he was? He would have to know that Vinnie would ultimately resurface and prove that he lied."

"Ok, well it doesn't matter if he thought he was dead or not if he lied. To me and Angelo, this seems like a setup. Like he was supposed to be killed and it just didn't work out that way."

"Why would Dino have Vinnie killed, he's a good man?"

"Because he's getting greedy. We started this to raise money to take back the neighborhood again when you come home and to help get your early parole guaranteed, but he doesn't give a shit about that. All he cares about is making money. He collects everything, I think he's taking his cut then skimming off of the top."

"Well, telling Vinnie to pretend to be dead was smart. He's an old man who seems to have lost his way, your right, maybe he's no longer trustworthy. I'm out of here in just under a year. I'll take care of it when I get out. Tell Vinnie to get out of town for now and strengthen that leg, and don't worry about anything. I want you guys to make sure his cut gets sent to him after every job."

"How the fuck am I going to swing that?" How am I going to convince Dino to pay out a dead man's half and where do I tell him it's going?"

Dino is old school. He may not be trustworthy anymore but he still understands respect. Tell him Vinnie died doing a job for me and I want his cut sent to his mother. Dino cannot refuse this gesture."

"And if he does?"

"If he does, well, then this wasn't accidental."

"What if he refuses to pay?"

"Then split all profits between the four of us and send him my portion. I'm doing ok here, I'll be fine until I get out."

"OK, but what do we do until you're out? I'm going to end up shot or arrested fucking with this old man. He cannot be trusted, and I don't want to take the chance of waiting another year to move on this."

"Just watch for the signs, they're easy to see once you know what you're looking for. Neither you nor Angelo works with Dino alone. Either both go or neither. Let him do his jobs and you two do yours. Just stay away as much as you can without becoming suspicious. Your main task is to get Vinnie out of town without Dino finding out."

The Nation

ONCE AGAIN, THE Zulu Nation has no leader. Yano calls for the members who are in line for the top seat and comes to them for a serious meeting. They are each discouraged and have mixed feelings about meeting with Yano, though they all show up.

"I have very few words for you men gathered here today. I have less than one year left in this place and I want to make it a peaceful year so my parole hearing does not become affected. I want no more quarrels with you men, but I promise that if anyone of you come at me again like you did when Franky lost his life, I will kill you all. Even if that means I have to stay another ten years. I don't want that to happen though. So I am here to make a peace offering. I am extending an olive branch, half of the drug trade back upon my release if this next year goes smoothly."

All of the men look around at each other, waiting for someone to speak. They all know that they could call a full out war and win, they could simply kill every Italian and take back one hundred percent of the drug trade. They have the manpower to do so, however, they have not had much luck in prior attempts. The Italians, though fewer, are stronger and smarter. They always come out on top.

"Franky was a good man and a great friend. It hurt me deeply when he died and I did not receive as much satisfaction as I hoped when I peeled apart the man responsible."

Yano begins to become emotional.

"You dumb jungle bunnies keep messing up. Why do you think you all keep dying? Why do you have to constantly recruit? It's because you constantly try to fight with us and with yourselves at the same time. You have no parameters. You elect a new leader, he says hit the Italians and then both your hitter and leader die. Now you're right back in the same place, no leader and a few men less. Eventually, you will kill yourselves off. I wish Marty didn't have to die. I sometimes think that he was the only smart man in your bunch. He knew how to conduct business. I grow tired so I am going to be done now, but if you believe me to be a joke, well, just try me. Make your move now, but I swear on the eyes of my little brother, it will only take one man, one incident, and we will go to war, and you will lose."

Every man left there was nervous. They all believe Yano's threat. They all know that he is not a man with empty words. He is a man who takes action and doesn't say anything that he doesn't mean. They now know that if they want to hit Yano, it must be big. The attack must be so massive that ever black man in the person would have to hit an Italian. The attack must be so precise, so swift, so well thought out, that Yano nor the family could ever recover from it. So, they called their meeting. The thirteen remaining men from Jaybird's meeting stood in a circle. They all agreed that the need for a new boss must be put on hold, for now, their organization must be run as a council. Yano was right, another attack was coming, but he had no idea how big it was going to be.

Now What?

VINNIE HAD BEEN released fro the hospital on a cool breezy day. He immediately went to the bus station and caught a train to Chicago to stay with his Aunt. Vinnie was not the type of man who would even think of going against anything Yano said to do. He was angered but trusted Yano, and he knew that he was not being pushed out of the family. That someday he would be allowed to return, but for now, he needed to concentrate on getting that leg better. Gino kept the secret, even Angelo was led to believe that Vinnie was dead, for a while. Gino did not want to run the risk of Dino overhearing anything, so Gino waited until he knew for sure that they were alone to fill Angelo in.

When Gino brought up the fact that Vinnie's portion of al future profits would go to Vinnie's family, Dino flipped out.

"There ain't no way in hell were sending twenty percent of my money to some dead kids family!"

"Our money!" Angelo screamed back.

"It's our money, Dino. This is not a game and its not a career that we're making here. It's a fundraiser. We're raising money for guns and ammunition and anything else that we need to free Yano. This is technically Yano's money! It's not for you to run out and buy a new car or something. You think we're out here doing this shit because we want to? No! Because we have to, we have no other means of income! Gino and I will take care of all the money from the trucks we boost. You can continue doing whatever the fuck you're doing. Keep all the jewel jobs and those risks for yourself you greedy old bastard.

"For real, Dino. What the hell is your problem? Vinnie was one of us and now he's gone. We should show enough respect for his memory to help out his family. If you want to be that disrespectful, then I'll fuckin bury you myself you piece of shit!"

Gino was not as good at keeping his cool like his brother. He was already ready to murder Dino and bring Vinnie back, but he knew that he couldn't for two reasons. The first being that Yano would be furious and the second being that with his knee the way it was, Vinnie was useless to them. Gino sees the signs that Yano spoke of. Dino is phony. Gino wants to react but acting without an unthought out plan could get him killed or thrown into prison, and Gino just doesn't understand that. The entire time they were yelling at Dino, he sat at his desk. He was nervous but he had his finger on the trigger of a loaded pistol, waiting for one of them to act. This is not how Dio wants things to play out so he agrees to pay Vinnie's family his cut and instructs them both to stay out of his way.

Day after day, week after week, there was an awkwardness between the three. Dino was nervous, he wasn't sure if the other two believed what he said happened to Vinnie. If they don't, then will they retaliate? If so, how and when? Gino and Angelo went about there business, robbing trucks. Neither ever spoke about Dino nor his actions, however, they both thought about it a lot. Is Dino going to try to take them out of the picture? Vinnie was gone about a month before things even began to feel normal again, but all three still walked on eggshells around each other.

As the three sat at the warehouse, a loud siren came smashing through their silence. The sound of a firetruck squealing its sirens down the street. All three jumps up and follow to see what was happening. As they rush down the street and around the corner, they are surprised when they see a two-story building with flames almost a hundred feet above the roof. Flames shooting from every window, the doors crackled from within. Screams could be heard over the breathing of the fire, loud and painful screams. Almost three hundred people trapped inside left to burn alive. The sound of death once again flood the air of this little Italian neighborhood of Omaha.

Angelo looks over at Gino.

"Is your mom at home today?"

"No, she's at work."

Suddenly he realizes why Angelo asked, it is the clinic in which she works that is so rapidly turning to ash. His heart falls to the floor as a tear builds in his eye. Gino drastically begins tearing through the crowd looking for his mother. The feeling of doubtful hope that she was able to escape kept running through his mind. Gino grabbed arms and spun bodies around, disappointed when he saw the many faces that were not his mother. Finally, he sees a man that he recognizes. It's one of the doctors that work at the clinic.

"Hey, did my mom get out in time? Please tell me she's not in there still."

The man has no response, he simply looks at Gino but only sees memories of the people burning alive as he fled the building.

"It blew up, it just blew up. No warning and no reason. This fire started hugely and is ending even bigger. It was like a bomb or something."

"Is my mother in there or not!"

"Yes, I saw her helping a man off of the floor as I fled. I never saw her exit the building though."

Gino was furious that the man escaped so quickly without trying to help anybody but himself, but now is not the time to deal with it. Angelo hollers at Gino. Once he gets his attention, he points to the back of the crowd. Four big men in suits stand laughing. Blackhand members, laughing at the screams of the innocent. Gino rushes over to them with only one intention, murder. Dino quickly jumps from between a couple of other guys and grabs Gino before he is spotted by the large Italian foes. He points out the fact that there are multiple cops as well as witnesses in the area and that Gino would never get away with anything.

"Think!" Dino says.

"They need to die! My mother is burning in there! I have to kill them!"

"I know you do, but it has to be done smart."

"Why? Do you think I care about prison? Yano would want me to do this!"

"Yes! Yes, he would but he would want you to do it smartly. If you go over there you could be killed yourself. What fuckin' good would that do? They could be laughing at something completely unrelated, then you go to prison forever for nothing. Just like with Enzo's murder, it has to be done right. Like Spilotti. Remember Spilotti? Remember how easy it was to kill him unnoticed? Or Scarpone? Paladino? Talapini? Do it smartly so the right people die and you will be free to live another day. You don't even know for sure if Fina is dead, let's concentrate on that for now."

"And if she is?"

"Then we kill them. We kill them all this time, but right now Rosaria needs you to be smart."

Once his sister is mentioned, Gino knows that Dino is right. Right now it almost feels as if Dino cared for Gino. He starts to wonder if maybe Dino did not have Vinnie clipped, but just got scared and took off as he said. The fact that he later lied about certain details are still there and confuse Gino. All he knows is that right then, when Dino said 'trust me', Gino trusted him.

"How the hell am I going to tell Yano that mom is dead?"

This news would surely kill anyone incarcerated, all hopes of one day seeing someone again ripped from your grasp for all eternity. Never having the chance to say goodbye or I'm sorry. After nine years of incarceration, Yano has a lot to say to his mother that he will never get the chance to say now. He doesn't take this news lightly.

"I never got the chance to say I love you, or goodbye, and I saw her every damn day. I can't imagine how he's going to feel."

"Gino," Dino begins, "If you're thinking about keeping this a secret from him until his release, I promise it's a bad idea. He will find out somehow, best it comes from you."

"I would never keep this from him, but at the same time, I don't want to tell him."

"Well do you have any family outside of this neighborhood anywhere? For what needs to happen next, Rosaria needs to go away. She isn't safe here and it's only going to get worse."

"Yeah, I have a place where she can go."

It won't be a family member's house. All of Gino's family are still back in Sicily. He will send his sister to stay with Vinnie.

And Then

AS YANO SITS in the yard, propped up on a weight bench, a number of his men stand around him. Yano needs as much protection as possible right now, he doesn't know if his words got through to the Nation and they can be as dangerous as they are unpredictable. Yano is not sure if his threat was deadly enough to scare them off, was his proposition of giving them back part of the drug trade worth it, or did it just piss them off and insult them? Until he knows which way they are leaning, he realizes that he needs to stay on his toes, but he's about to find out a lot sooner than anticipated. Words are yelled, and then lots of movement.

"Squash them!"

Every black man in the yard heard these words and began rushing the Italians. Italians were caught off guard so badly that they barely had any time to react. Rocko picks up a ten-pound weight and begins swinging it around. Most of the blacks were armed with homemade prison shanks and only a few Italians had anything but their fists. Few were close enough to grab a weight near the bench. There were just too many people running around with murder as an intent, Yano and his men could not keep an eye on everybody. They were forced to just fight who was ever near them and pray that they had a friend watching their backs.

Rocko swings his weight and nails a man in the face. Blood and a few teeth pieces fly from the man's mouth as a loud cracking sound echoes from his now shattered jaw. As he cocked his arm back to swing again, another man came from his blindside and sticks a shard into his gut. As Rocko falls to his knees he understands that a lot of people are destined to die today.

Antonio has a hold of the weight bar. He sees Rocko fall and comes running and swinging his giant metal stick, laying down any man who was standing in front of him. One man had a skull collapse before he fell, another with a broken collar bone, and a third caught the bar across the spine, shattering multiple vertebrae. Antonio reaches Rocko in time to help him to his feet and get him out of the center of this death ring.

Yano is trapped. He has his back to a corner, nowhere to go. Three men are standing there swinging blades at him. Yano takes multiple cuts on the arms as he swings a big weight around as protection. He can only hope that he hits these men just right or he has some help get there soon. He doesn't feel as if he can swing this weight around too much longer, and he fears the sting of their blades will be felt quite soon. He swings a few more times, once cracking against one of the men's wrists. His hand broke and his blade fell. Yano makes a quick gesture as if someone is coming to help. Both of the last armed assailants fall for the bluff and look behind them. Yano takes this opportunity to grab the fallen blade and find it a home in one man's gut. Yano rocked the blade up and down and then began to twist it in a circular motion. Yano knows that this wound if a vital organ was hit, would be very hard to recover from. Before the man fell, Yano had a few men show up and handle the remaining man.

Antonio is pulling Rocko to the side where it is, not so much safe but, less dangerous. Two black guys run up behind him and puncture his back several times with their knives. Antonio screams and falls, almost on top of Rocko. Yano's two most trusted men are both down. The sirens begin screaming, as do the guards as they come running from the building.

"Get down! Everybody on the floor! Get the fuck down now!"

Most of the men involved were already lying on the ground dead, dying, or severely injured. Yano can escape around the corner and back inside the prison before the guards notice him. Yano runs through the door, down through the corridor, up the stairs, down the concourse area, and passed a cell that two Italian men are sitting in. These men are in complete oblivion to what was happening, they simply sat there playing cards.

"Give me a shirt and some pants. Now! Bring them to the shower."

Yano started running again tearing his shirt and pants from his body and throwing them into a nearby trashcan and in to the shower room. Once inside, he begins washing all of the blood from his arms and face. The cuts all over his arm are going to be impossible to hide from anyone. As Yano leaves the shower, he carries the towel in his wounded arm, trying to hide the cut marks. He exits the shower and walks right into the Warden.

"Well, I was just coming to find you. Didn't I tell you to keep your shit together?"

"What are you talking about, Warden? I haven't done anything."

"What do you call that fuckin' riot outside? Nothing?"

"Riot? Warden, I..."

"I don't want to hear your bull shit lies you fuckin wop! I told you to be good or I'd fuck you over. Now I have multiple dead bodies outside. What am I supposed to do? Just act like I didn't notice any of them?"

"Warden, I swear, I've been in the shower. I don't know anything about a riot. I'm no longer in charge of what those guys do. Their actions are just that, theirs. I cannot control what other inmates do."

"Oh don't give me that bull shit. I have to charge someone with all of these new murders and you're the one I warned. Looks like it's going to need to be you who falls on this sword."

The Warden turns to walk away when he is suddenly stopped by Yano's hand on his shoulder. Yano spins the Warden around, grabs him by the throat, and pushes him hard up against a wall.

"You better think twice about charging me with anything else."

Neither the Warden not Yano say anything else. Yano lets go and walks away. The Warden knows not to be afraid or upset. Yano gets about ten feet away when the Warden gets enough balls to mumble a few words.

"I know you're still in charge, Yano."

Yano stops and turns around slowly.

"You don't know shit, Warden."

"One of your men is in my office almost every day talking to me. I've known the entire time that you are still running shit. I only let it slide because nothing bad was happening, but now, after this, how can I let anything slide?"

"You're saying one of my men is a rat?"

All of Yano's men, from right-hand man to the lowest soldier, knew enough to get Yano a life sentence. The Warden refused to let the name slip so there was no real way to know who it was. Yano had a few of his guys begin surveillance missions. It needs to be a different man every day to avoid any suspicion. Yano is hoping that this is a bluff, but the warden never bluffs. If he says a man is talking then there's a man talking. Yano has zero ideas of who it could possibly be, but if there *is* a snitch, how could he be handled? No matter what or how anything happens to him the warden will know, he'll also know why. Yano starts to think that this is a set up to get him in more trouble. If there is a man with a loud mouth he can't just walk away, he has to be dealt with accordingly, but how? Yano is confused, this is going to take some careful planning. The warden is dead set on making Yano stay in prison longer, this setup would be a perfect way. The warden is not above putting a man in danger to fuck over Yano.

"Yano, you have a visitor."

Yano puts on his boots and leaves his cell. As he gets to the Visitation room he sees Gino.

"Where's mom? Why didn't she come with you?"

Gino, with tears in his eyes, explains what happened. He tells Yano of the fire, of the laughing Italians, and how Dino grabbed him and stop him from killing the man. Yano surprisingly took the news very well, not one tear fell down his cheek.

"Dino was right."

He tells Gino he shouldn't have left Rosaria alone. He should have brought her along. Gino begins to tell his brother how he sent her off to live with Vinnie. He told the other guys said she was staying with family.

"Vinnie and protect her better than any of us will be able to in this neighborhood. She had to go and she agreed. She left without a fight, she always liked Vinnie and had no problem going to stay with him. She stayed for mom's funeral and I took her to Vinnie's myself right after."

Yano nods, says nothing, just gets up and walks away. As he gets to the door he stops.

"That was good thinking. I trust Vinnie with my life, he's a good man."

Yano opens the door, turns to Gino and says,

"I love you,"

then turns back and leaves.

Two of Yano 's men were killed in the outside brawl, thirteen more wounded. Seven black men died and only four wounded. Yano had to put his words into actions now, he told them that if they made another move, that he would bury them all. Now he must follow through with it, now is the time for action. The time for words is over.

Yano's brain and nerves were on an emotional overload. His mother's death, her vengeance, Rosaria's safety, the rat, and the warden trying to set him up were all on his mind. All the time, all at once. Now he has a mass murder attack to plan. This was too much for an average twenty-eight-year-old man to worry about. However, Yano was not an average twenty-eight-year-old man. He is the boss. Not a CEO of a huge corporation, but the boss of a criminal organization and these are the things a boss like that has to deal with, constantly. Competition and how to deal with it. This is the life he chose, but this is not the life he was supposed to have. He wasn't born into those like the Blackhand members. He was forced into it. He has no choice but to keep business going and with all this fighting, he is losing money. Money that he needs to properly fight the Blackhand upon his release, so he cannot spend his time mourning the loss of his mother. No matter how bad he feels he has to clear his head, he has to deal with the problems at hand. His brother and sister are the only family he has left, he needs to fix these problems, get as much money as he can, and get home to keep them safe. So, for now, he sits alone and thinks.

It's been two weeks since the assault on the Italians and Rocko was finally being released from the medical wing. The blade pierced his lung just slightly but he was going to be fine. He explains that with his injuries the Warden restricted him to light duties and he was moved to kitchen work. He also tells Yano that before, when he was doing janitorial work, he saw a box of rat poison being used in the basement.

"I can get into the basement and get that poison. We can use it to our advantage somehow."

Yano agrees and sends him to retrieve it. A few minutes after he leaves, a guard yells out "Supper time! Everyone to the chow Hall!"

A lightbulb quickly shines over Yano's head as he has an idea. It's crazy, but it just might be crazy enough to work. he explains the plan to Rocko.

"I'll get the word out to Antonio and the rest of the guys."

That night Yano speaks worth Antonio. Antonio starts to laugh uncontrollably as Yano tells him what's going on. As he starts to calm down he agrees to the plan and quickly starts spreading the word to all of his men. Only two hours later a man named Paulie Malone comes to Yano.

"I've been keeping an eye on the warden's office as you instructed me to." Pauli continues, "No one has spotted me, but I spotted someone else. The same man, a man by the name of Bruno Strazzi, has been visiting the warden damn near every day and he's there for about forty-five minutes each time so he must be talking. He's always there too long to be cleaning or doing any other kind of work. He's gotta be the rat, right? Do you know him, Yano?"

"Yeah, I know him. He was raped in the showers by some white boys when he first got here last year. He came to me for help but he came demanding that I help. He showed me complete disrespect so I sent him away, him being the rat would not surprise me. How much can this guy, this…outsider, really know about our business? He is not involved in the family so somebody must be telling him these things."

Pauli tells Yano that he isn't too sure, he has never spoken to Bruno before.

"Does he know of tomorrow's plans?"

Again, Pauli explains that he isn't sure.

"There's no real way to find out what all he has told the Warden."

Yano sighs, "Well, find out who he does talk to and bring them to me."

The Rat's Friend

YANO IS ON edge. He is nervous and beginning to feel as if he is about to lose everything. A rat is a treacherous being, but a smart rat is just as dangerous as he is treacherous. Yano also begins to wonder if he should quit while he's ahead, retire from the business, and pass the leadership onto Antonio, but he can't quit. There are too many people counting on him and he's not sure if Antonio has what it takes to be a good boss. The Nation also needs to be dealt with. Yano does not make idol threats. His words need to be placed into action or they will take advantage of this and assume Yano to be weak. No, quitting and walking away is not an option, even if that means prolonging his stay. Yano has to become twice as cautious. He needs to grow eyes in the back of his head.

Following directions, Pauli continues to follow Bruno. His source of information and what the Warden knows is important. Mostly to keep Yano safe from prolonging his stay, but also to ease his mind. Not knowing who all is talking is going to lead to Yano becoming paranoid, he won't know who to trust pretty soon and innocent people may end up getting clipped.

One day Pauli sees Bruno head into the shower room. He has no towel, no soap, no clean clothes, nothing. This seems a bit odd to Pauli, but within a few minutes, another empty-handed man enters. It's a meeting, a meeting of the rats, the rat, and his friend. What would the friend of a rat be? A snake? Another rat perhaps? The second man is not well known to Pauli but he is familiar. His name, Vito Ruggerio. He is the cousin of Yano's slain friend Frankie. Yano loved him like a brother and now Pauli has to tell Yano that it may be his cousin who is singing to Bruno.

Vito has never had any part of the family business, so how does he know anything? There must be yet another man involved, but who? The rat friend of the rat's friend? This is getting confusing. Pauli contemplates many things as the two men leave the shower and head in different directions. Pauli doesn't know which to follow so he continues tailing Bruno. Bruno goes to the chow hall then back to his cell, no more meetings for the night. So Pauli heads back to fill in Yano. As he is walking towards Yano's cell, the man in the neighboring cell jumps as he hears Pauli approaching. He seemed to be sitting awfully close to the wall. Just then Pauli notices something and a lightbulb clicks above his head.

"Yano, we need to take a walk."

The two exit the cell and head down the corridor.

"I found the snitches."

"Who?"

Well, besides Bruno? There's Vito Ruggerio."

"No! Frankie's cousin?"

"That's not all."

Pauli was nervous, how do you tell the boss that his neighbor is spying on him? How do you tell the boss of a criminal scarpenterprise that the information being leaked is coming straight from his mouth? How do you tell the boss of an ongoing murderous gang of convicts that he is the loudmouth?

"I caught Vito listening to your conversation."

"What conversation?"

"Whichever one you were just talking to Antonio and Rocko about."

"Tomorrow night's plans!" He has to be stopped, now. Before he can tell the Warden what we're about to do."

"That's why I didn't want to tell you back there, I don't want him to know that we're on to him."

"what do you think we should do?"

"You're the boss, Yano. You tell me. Whatever it is, I'm behind you."

"He has never wanted any part too what we do, yet, we have never had any problem with him. Why now?"

"He probably blames us for Frankie's death"

"His death is not our fault. His blood is not at my feet. He died for loyalty. I didn't force him to jump in front of that blade."

Pauli agrees and tries to console Yano but also reminding him that they do not have much time until Vito decides to squeal. Yano walks back into his cell and quickly places a finger over his mouth. He turns toward the desk and writes a little note, then hands it to Antonio and Rocko.

Do not speak about business here anymore. The rat's lair is next door.

Antonio and Rocko both look at each other in disbelief. Yano gestures to them and they all leave the cell and take a small walk as he fills them in on Pauli's findings.

"Never pay attention to what I speak of in that room anymore. It will be completely fabricated information to throw Vito off. If he notices that we have gone silent, he may decide its time to speak with the Warden."

Everybody is upset with Vito's disloyalty to the very people that his cousin gave his life for.

Rocko mumbles, "I think we need to just carry out our plans. Why put on a front for him?"

"I want him to hear and lead the warden away to a fictitious murder site. That way they won't be around when our real plan happens. Then we'll take care of both Vito and Bruno, but until then I want you guys to go talk about me. Say something about me going to kill some black men who are hiding in the basement gambling. Make sure he hears you. If the warden thinks that I'm about to kill some people myself he'll definitely go and try to catch me in the act. When he gets there the room will be empty. Then when he comes back, there will be dead cones everywhere. None of our people can be around when it happens, that way he can't pin it on us. Talk to the Irishmen, get them to do this for us."

As Rocco heads to the basement to retrieve the rat poison, Antonio heads to talk with the Irish. Afterward, they both meet back up at Yano's cell.

"Did you hear what's going on tonight?" Antonio started.

"No."

"Yano heard that some niggers are going to sneak downstairs for something later. Yano is already down there waiting for them."

"Why? What's he going to do?"

"What the hell do you think? He's going to kill them."

Vito's ear is pushed up as close to the wall as he could get.

"Yano hates the blacks for killing Franky. His retaliation against them will never be finished."

Why is he doing it himself?"

"I don't know, I told him I would do it for him, but he insists. This is personal to him."

As the two conspire against Vito, Pauli shows up. He hears the two men talking and gets upset that they are still speaking about business in there after Yano told them to stop. He was unaware that it was a setup. Antonio hushes Pauli and the three of them walk down the hall. Rocco takes one look back and sees Vito flee. He is definitely in a hurry to get somewhere.

The Irish are all on board with this plan. They had been pushed around by the Nation for a long time, it was time to fight back. The plan was approved by Irish leaders, and their ideas would also be implemented. All details were in order, and everyone who played a role and needed to know knew. The Irish went to work and began to set the plan into motion.

Snitching

BRUNO AND VITO arrived at the Warden's office minutes before the guards called for supper. Yano was right, the Warden quickly gathered a few guards and rushed downstairs.

"That stupid fuckin' wop. I knew he couldn't stay out of trouble. I got him now."

As they rushed towards the basement to catch Yano, an Irishman went to work in the kitchen. The entire kitchen staff, but one, were all black. This is what made the plan so good. When the cooks were not looking, the Irishman dropped the entire box of rat poison into the huge pot of mashed potatoes. Anyone who was not supposed to die was given warnings to stay away from the mess hall tonight. The people who showed up for dinner were in trouble.

The Warden kicked the door open and sees nothing but an empty room. The guards search but find nothing. Everyone is confused. Another guard comes running, yelling at the Warden from the top of the stairs.

"Hey! You need to come and see this!"

As they rush to the cafeteria, the Warden knew he had been deceived. They reach the chow hall and notice close to one hundred men who were, a few short minutes ago enjoying a meal, but now, on the floor dying. The victims were mainly black, however, some were Hispanic, and some untrustworthy Italians and Irishman. Such a wide variety of victims left the suspected assailant a mystery. The Warden wanted to believe that this was Yano's doing, however, he could never prove it. Italian and Irish rats were left to die, along with inmates who had committed crimes against women and children. This is what made the scene so confusing. Yano made a deal with the Irish that his business' would be turned over to them upon Yano's release. The Irish knew that with the Nation damn near eliminated, the only ones left to fight them for it would be the Hispanics. So they decided to take them out now while they were still unsuspecting of anything.

The Warden ran out to the hall and saw Yano and some friends joking around with a few guards.

"You god damn wop! I know this was you! You've really overstepped this time!"

Yano looked confused as he argued with the Warden.

"I have no idea what you're talking about. What did I supposedly do this time?"

"You know god damn well what happened! This is the worst crime ever committed in this facility since I've been here! In all my thirty years, I have never seen anything so atrocious!"

Yano swears that he has been standing there with the guards the entire time, and the guards all swear that Yano was nowhere near the cafeteria recently.

"My source tells me that your buddy Antonio was overheard telling Rocco that you were heading to the basement to kill some niggers! Why would they tell me that? And then coincidentally the basement is empty but a massacre takes place one floor up? Your name is involved in everything!"

"I never said anything like that! To Rocco, or to anyone else. Your source is a fuckin' liar!"

"Why would he lie? What would he gain from making that up?"

Yano responds, "Oh I don't know, guaranteed parole? A few years shaved off of his sentence? You tell me, Warden, what did you promise this guy to make him turn rat? We all know that you like to make suspicious promises to inmates."

"I'm going to prove this was you somehow, Yano!"

The Warden stomps off, furious. He knows that he can't prove anything, there's nothing to pin on Yano or anyone else for this crime. He is going to have to answer to his higher-ups and will have no answers to give. It is his ass on the line now so he is going to be up Yano's ass more now than ever. The guards all tell Yano how they don't believe he had anything to do with this and they were willing to testify to the parole board on Yano's behalf. The guards can see the vindictive side the Warden has been slowly developing.

"We can testify on your behalf, this time. We all know that you have done some evil shit since you've been in here Yano. We can't prove it, but we're not dumb. If they ask us about anything else, we'll have no choice but to address it honestly."

"And by honestly, do you mean to give your opinion of what you believe happened? Or do you mean to show factual evidence to prove that I did something?"

"Well like we said, we can't prove anything, but we all know you did it. It would be too much of a coincidence that Smith, for example, tried to go to war with you and he ended up dead. Or what about the riots that happened that the Italians were involved in? What about all assaults against the black inmates that lead to retaliatory assaults against Italians? As I said, we're not stupid."

"It is true that Italians and the blacks have been going back and forth for a while, but if you cant prove that I instigated any of it, or took any part in any crime, then I'd really appreciate that you keep your mouths shut. All you'll be doing is smearing my name without evidence and we all know that the parole board doesn't need evidence to make their decision. So you could be dooming me to stay here longer for things that I had nothing to do with. My name is only involved in situations because you have a suspicion that I was involved. Is that enough to make me stay here longer? Before you answer that, keep in mind what happens to my supposed enemies or people who betray me."

The guards aren't stupid. They know that Yano is threatening their well-being. They also know that he is right. Their suspicions aren't enough to keep Yano incarcerated longer than need be. The threats bother the guards but Yano intended them to be more of a reminder of who he is and what he is capable of more than meaning them as a direct threat. Either way, the guards got the message.

Questions

BACK AT HOME, Gino sits on his bed, looking at old photo albums. As he stares at what used to be, he wonders what could have been. What would their lives look like today had they never left Sicily? Would Enzo have been murdered? His father, taken from him far too soon. Never to teach his sons what it takes to be a man. Never to teach them how to shave, or how to drive. His mother, Fina, murdered. Also taken to soon. A son needs a mother as much as he needs his father. A mother's love to give them that certain sensitivity that a man needs to nurture a wife and a baby of his own. Would they still be dead? Maybe not murdered, but by the disease that the poor lands of Sicily held.

What of Yano? Would he still be taken away from his brother, forcing them to grow into men separately? Would they still be turned into teenage killers? Would their baby sister be forced into hiding still? Would he be living at his mother and father's home all alone? What of his friends? What would their lives look like if the Scarpacci family hadn't come to Omaha? Would Vincent Marino's leg be torn apart by bullets? Would Dino Ganapini soon be facing a death sentence or still running a small-time casino? What about little Irish Patrick? Would he be dead? Would Antonio Carusso ever have killed a man and been sentenced to prison at such a young age?

A lot of lives were ruined because of Enzo's death. What of Don Talapini and his men? Would dozens of them lie dead or would they still be alive and tormenting small business owners in the neighborhood? How many innocent people had been murdered by Talapini's men and how many innocent lives spared by the initial death of the Black Hand? This thought brought Gino some comfort, along with knowing that he would soon be responsible for saving more lives once Yano returns. Then they will be able to start to pick apart what remains of the Black Hand. Gino had to lose his family in order for others to keep theirs. This was his sacrifice, though, he doesn't understand why it had to be his family. Why did it have to be Yano that was taken from him? Why were these two brothers chosen to clean up the neighborhood?

When he had finally gotten to the point in which his eyes were so full of tears he couldn't look at another photo, he quit trying to understand the why. He knows that things are not going to change. He can not bring back his parents, he has to accept that. He knows that one day soon, Yano will return and they would begin doing whatever was needed to bring Rosaria home. As Gino was leaving the house, he was realizing that now is the time to start thinking about the people who could be brought back instead of the ones who couldn't.

Gino heads down to Dino's to meet the guys, along with a guy named Tommy D'Agusta, a parolee from Yano's crew who had just come home. Yano had the idea to send his best men home to meet Gino upon their release, to help with the Blackhand. As Gino arrived, he didn't even pay attention to the new face.

"Are we still waiting for Yano to get home, or can we start this shit already?"

"I think we should," Angelo explains. "but things are going to keep getting worse before they get any better so I'd, personally, rather not. Maybe we can start securing a source of guns, at least for now, it's a start."

Dino adds, "The next time you go visit him, you can speak with him and get his input. I think once we get armed, we can attack, but I also really want to wait for Yano. This is something we started together and I think we should finish it together. I mean, he's only got ten months left, but a lot of bad shit can happen in ten months. It wouldn't be the smartest idea to wait."

"Well," Gino starts, "I've been thinking, and I want to attack tonight."

"Hell no! There's no way we can," Angelo replies, "We're nowhere near prepared to start tonight."

"I didn't say I was going to, just that I want to. I'm getting impatient, we need to do something. The people in the neighborhood used to be so scared to even come outside, until we took care of Talapini's men. Remember how that all changed after the fire? It was great for so long but everyone is quickly giving in to the fear again."

"Don't you think Yano might want to relax when he gets home? Maybe just enjoy being out? After all, he's finishing up a ten-year sentence."

Gino looks at Tommy as he speaks and giggles.

"No, and who the fuck are you? What do you know about my brother?"

"Sorry, my name's Tommy, and I know your brother very well. I was locked up for six years with him and he is my hero. He did something in there that no Italian has ever done before and put us at the top of the food chain. Italians used to be targeted until he arrived, then we became the most dangerous people in the prison. My point is, though, that maybe he's tired of it."

"My brother turned himself from a small town Sicilian killer to a fucking boss of an entire criminal organization, a break is the last thing he's going to want. He's not going to live that way for so long then come home and quit. This all started because these fucks murdered our father and as long as our vengeance needs to be handed out, he will not rest, and I don't want there to be a year worth of work to do before we strike when he gets out. When he gets released, I want to be ready to go. We have money from truck heists saved up, let's buy some fuckin guns and then figure out how we can secure his parole."

"What about getting him out even earlier?" Tommy stated.

"Hold that thought," Gino says, "Do you remember Jonny Eyes, Angelo?"

"Yeah."

"Maybe he can get us guns. He sells drugs so he must have a way to protect himself. We don't even need a lot of guns, just a few with a lot of bullets. Do you still have his contact info?"

I'll check."

As Angelo goes to look for Jonny's phone number, Gino turns back to Tommy and asks him about his last comment. Getting Yano released earlier seemed almost impossible to Gino. Tommy explains to him that he was just recently paroled and that it was his third parole meeting before he was finally granted. Tommy says that with all three meetings, there was always one thing in common. One man, a committee member who was in charge of all three meetings. Chances are pretty good that he'll be in charge of Yano's as well. If they could get to this man somehow, maybe they could blackmail him into releasing Yano.

Gino couldn't believe what he was hearing. He had never contemplated extortion before, but at a young age, he buried his father, became a murderer, watched his brother get shot and arrested, sent his sister to hide from dangerous people, and then buried his mother. Is extortion really that bad? It depends on what is involved, he thinks.

As the two of them talk about how they can secure Yano's parole, Yano was dealing with the fallout of the mess hall massacre. One hundred and eight people were the final victim count. Involved were eighteen Hispanics, twenty-two Irishman, twenty-one Italians, and forty-seven Nation members. The Irish targeted the Hispanics as the Italians targeted the Nation. That leaves sixty-five targets hit as well as forty-three snitches, turncoats, criminals against children, and other undesirables are also taken care of. None of them would be missed and Yano was happy with the results of this mass attack. The Nation suffers from it's least number of members in the history of their organization and they are at their weakest point.

Two more people need to die that managed to avoid the cafeteria, Vito Ruggerio and Bruno Strazzi. After these two last hits, Yano should be in the clear. There will be nobody left talking, nobody left to fight. He will finally have time to just sit back and relax. Maybe he can finally mourn his mother's death properly, but first, he decides to take a nap. The stress that he has been under for so long has left him tired. Yano lay down and didn't rise again until the next day. The voice of a guard yelling out that he has a visit is what finally broke his slumber.

Gino tells Yano that they require weapons and they are starting to get a plan put in place.

"I can get you Jonny Eye's number, but you have to contact him yourself. After what just happened in here, I cannot make that type of phone call."

"Well, won't you see him soon? You can talk with him in person."

"He doesn't drop off the next shipment until next month, he was just here a week ago."

"Yeah, we can't wait another month."

"Gino, you need to be careful out there. I can be out in ten months if I get parole. I don't want anything happening to you before I get back home."

"It's ok, Yano. I got people watching my back. I got Angelo and Dino and Tommy. We also met up with the new guy Carlo, that you just sent us. I'm not too sure about Dino, but when he's gone Vinnie can come home."

"Be careful with Carlo. He was always a loyal soldier in here, but I have always had a funny feeling about him."

"What do you mean?"

"Like his loyalty can be bought. As I said, he was always loyal to me, but just keep an eye on him. Just in case."

As Gino left the prison, he stopped at the first payphone he saw to contact Jonny and set up a meet. Angelo was told about this and decided to accompany Gino just in case Jonny has other plans. He is loyal to Yano, but Angelo and Gino do not know him, nor do they trust him. As the two pull up and meet Jonny, they notice that he also brought a friend along. Gino walks up to him and begins to speak, but before he can get out three words, Jonny cuts him off.

Wait, I am not a gun runner. So unless you need some sort of narcotic, then you need to speak with this man. He is a friend of mine, names are not important, but he's the one who can help you. He doesn't trust you, but I told him that I've been doing business with your brother for a long time now and that you are stand up guys. So don't make me look like a liar."

"What do you fellows need?"

"Guns. Something powerful and reliable. About ten of them. We need a lot of bullets. Nothing cheap that will jam up, price doesn't matter, we want the best. We're not your average stick up kids, we need something that we can take to war."

Gino explained everything without getting too much into detail about their intended targets.

"Well, I got just what you need. I have a dozen Thompson submachine guns. These work in all weather conditions and never jam up. They are capable of killing thirty people per second, real hardcore firepower. The thing is, I sell by quantity. If you want these, then you'll have to take all twelve. I can't do shit with two leftovers, and honestly, it isn't even worth the effort trying."

"I expect that this weapon will not leave me fucked will it? I don't want it to brake in the middle of a gunfight."

"Are you kidding me? This is the most popular assault weapon on the market right now. It holds fifty rounds per drum and never jams up. They are a little on the expensive side but well worth it if you plan on using them more than once or twice. You talk about going to war, well I wouldn't trust going to war with anything else."

"How much do you want for them, and when can we expect delivery?"

"Shit man, whenever you want. They're in my warehouse right now. I can let you have these plus the pistols you want for thirty-five hundred. Make it an even four thousand and I'll give you all the ammo I got. That's about four thousand rounds for the Tommys and a thousand for the pistols. If that's not enough for a small war, I can look into getting you more."

Gino and Angelo talk it over. Neither knows how much they should be paying, neither knows if this man is ripping them off. They both do know that they need these and they have enough to pay for it, so they agree.

"can you deliver them? We have a warehouse right outside little Italy. You know Dino right? We're at his place."

"Yeah, I know Dino. I didn't know you were with him though, why didn't he come?"

"He doesn't know we're here."

"Ok, we can meet you at his spot tonight."

"Good, I also have a little more business I would like to speak with you about."

Gino and Jonny walk away and speak of other things as Angelo and the gunman talk about the details of the delivery.

It only took a few hours and Jonny and his friend were knocking at the warehouse door. Dino opens up and is surprised to see Jonny.

"We forgot to tell you that we had a shipment coming in Dino," Angelo says as he and Gino walk in through the back.

Dino opens the big door and Jonny's friend drives the truck in.

"What did you boys get us?"

Dino begins to pick through the shipment and gets excited to see the Tommy guns and pistols.

"Holy shit! That's a lot of ammunition. Well, boys, I'd say we're about ready."

"Hey Dino," Jonny mutters, "You gonna tell us what is going on? Or is it top secret?"

Dino smiles, he knows he shouldn't say anything, but he sits the boys down and explains it all from the beginning. Afterward, Jonny stands up and walks to the back room to speak with Gino.

"You were right. He opened right up like a highschool girl spittin' gossip. He told us everything."

"Yeah, I'm not surprised. Let's do this."

"You sure Yano is ok with this?"

"Fuck that, it needs to be done. I'll explain it to Yano later."

Gino hands over the money for the guns, plus a little more. As they walk back into the front room they can hear Dino laughing. He is telling him the details of the diner burning down and how the innocent people ended up being burnt alive. He thought it was the funniest part of the story. As he continues, Gino and Jonny walk up to the truck and pick up a pistol. Jonny turns around and shoots three shots into Dino's chest. Before Dino could hit the ground three more shots fire from Gino's barrel. All three settling in the face of Carlo. Carlo is dead before he hits the floor, but Dino, Dino lays there gasping.

Angelo walks up to Dino and tells him that they know the truth about Vinnie. Just before he shoots the final bullet into Dino's head, he tells him that Vinnie is still alive and that they all knew that he conspired to have Vinnie killed.

Dino is dead. Gino and Angelo stand there quietly looking at one another. Jonny smiles. His friend is freaked out because he was unaware that any of this was going to happen. Jonny nods at Gino, sets the pistol down, and the two exit the warehouse. Gino and Angelo begin to clean up and develop a story to tell Yano.

The Next Step

DINO IS GONE. As is Carlo. Nobody misses Carlo since they didn't even know him, but Dino, how could it have gotten to this point? Dino was a big part of Gino's life, a sort of mentor after their father died. Gino knew that Dino was changing and that he had to go before he put anybody else in jeopardy as he did to Vinnie, but it's still hard for him to deal with. Having killed Dino brought tremendous stress upon Gino, how was he to explain this to Yano?

As Gino headed to the prison to speak with his brother he thought over and over of what to say but no words came to him. He had to tell Yano before he found out another way that Dino and his friend Carlo had been killed. Gino enters the prison, nervous, shaky. As he entered the visitation room Yano was already there.

"How you doing bro?" Yano started.

"Not too good."

Yano looks at his little brother confused.

"You need to sit down, we need to talk."

As Gino began speaking, the words just fell from his mouth. The lie came so easily you could've sworn that he had practiced it.

"Dino and Carlo got into an argument. They're both dead."

Yano freaked out as Carlo was a great soldier and a good guy. As Gino explained to Yano that the two had a beef ever since Carlo first arrived, Yano's eyes began to swell. Gino couldn't tell if this was more because of Carlo's or Dino's death.

"What were they arguing about?"

"We're not entirely sure. By the time we heard the shots, it was too late."

Yano stood up and began to pace back and forth.

"That's not all, Yano."

"What else could there possibly be?"

"Dino was running his mouth about everything that had happened. The diner, Gianni, Talapini, and everything that we are getting ready to do."

"Running his mouth to who?"

"Jonny and a friend of his that we bought our gun supply from. I don't know how well you know Jonny, Yano, but we cannot have any outsiders knowing our business."

This is Gino's way of trying to rid the world of Jonny Eyes, the only guy who could tell Yano the truth about Dino and Carlo. Gino needed to tie up loose ends.

"Well, I'm about out of product. Let me contact Jonny and order a couple of month's worth, and then you guys do whatever you feel needs done."

Gino and Yano finish their visit talking about their parents and that time they spent the day at the beach right before leaving Sicily. When Gino walked out of prison, he had a slight grin. He cannot believe that he pulled this off so smoothly. Not only that, but know he has permission to eliminate Jonny and his friend. There is one other thing that must be done though. Gino knows that Angelo would never speak the truth to Yano about what happened, but what about Tommy? Gino doesn't know him and doesn't trust him. Something has to happen to Tommy. He has to go away.

Yano contacts Jonny and tells him he needs to re-up on supplies. Jonny, ecstatic that Yano needs so much, tells him that there's no way that he could get that much into him at once. He says that he will have to come two days in a row.

"Make it three." Yano tels him.

Yano is expecting to have enough dope to last his final ten months. This is his only source of income at the moment so he had to get as much as possible before Jonny disappears.

Gino tells Angelo that Yano had given his blessing to take out Jonny.

"How the hell are we going to do this though? We don't know Jonny's friend's name nor where to find him?"

Angelo reassures Gino that it wouldn't be too hard.

"We'll just order another shipment of ammo and when they show, well, they won't walk out again."

"What about Tommy?'

Angelo begins to zone out into space. He begins to worry. Not so much about Tommy, he knows that leaving him alive is a liability, and seeing as he was the one to put the final bullet into Dino's face, he damn sure doesn't want Yano to find out the truth. He worries about Gino. Gino is beginning to let his head swell. He seems as if he doesn't care who he kills anymore, as if he is only thinking about himself. Angelo can't help but wonder how far Gino is willing to go to protect this secret. Could Angelo's life be in danger? He has known Gino for years and doesn't want to believe that Gino would turn on him, but would he? Angelo doesn't let Gino know that he is thinking this way. He just plays his role and keeps an eye on the situation.

"Angelo!"

Angelo jumps back to reality, "Yeah?"

"What about Tommy?"

"Well, I think I have a plan. You go grab Jonny's number and give him a call. Order a couple of hundred dollars worth of ammo and get them down here."

"We don't have the money to pay for that!"

"I know, that's why we're not going to pay for it."

"Ahh, I got you, but we can't call him today. We have to wait until Yano is done with him."

"It took forever to clean up after we killed Dino and Carlo, I don't want to fuck with that again," Gino says.

Angelo agrees. The next day Jonny goes to the prison, as he said he would. Angelo and Gino decide to drive up there also. They want to follow Jonny back to his neighborhood in hopes of finding a better dumpsite. They watch as Jonny enters with a briefcase, and then approximately a half an hour later exit without it. It is the middle of the day and they are not willing to kill Jonny right now and leave any witnesses. They have to be smart. They do not want to make any mistakes so close to Yano getting released.

As they follow Jonny home, they notice a few places that would be a great dumpsite. A bridge that they need to drive over, with virtually no houses around. It's secluded and goes right over the river. They could dump the bodies in there, they thought.

Day two, the two boys drive back to Jonny's neighborhood. This is the day that they are going to make them disappear. As they enter the neighborhood, they notice Jonny walking with another briefcase. They both thought that he was on his way to make another delivery but were unaware that Yano was on the receiving end again. They followed the car, waiting for a good place to strike. They end up following Jonny back to the prison. Yano receives two out of three packages as planned. If the second delivery was unknown to the boys, so was the third. They followed Jonny back to his neighborhood not knowing that they were about to fuck Yano over.

As Jonny was driving, things began to get a little more complicated. Jonny dozed off while driving, he coasted into the oncoming traffic lane and almost sideswiped a police car. As the cop turned around to pull Jonny over, Jonny took off. Gino and Angelo follow them both from a safe distance so the cop doesn't notice them. The cop is finally able to get close enough to Jonny's car and bump their bumpers together. When this happened, Jonny's car spun. He spun multiple times before he finally came to a stop. Jonny exits his vehicle and instantly starts shooting. A long gunfight pursued. Jonny finally runs out from behind his car and tries to shoot, but he runs out of ammo. The cop rushes at him and tackles him to the ground. As the boys watch as Jonny is placed in cuffs they realize that this is a bad situation. They believe Jonny will snitch and he has great info to do so with.

Gino drives up closer and slams on the breaks. As the cop puts Jonny in the back seat, Gino ran up to the car and unloads his weapon. He shot every bullet he had through the back window, hitting Jonny multiple times throughout the body. As the cop turns and aims his pistol at Gino, Angelo approached. The cop gets off one shot, hitting Gino in the arm. Angelo then unloaded his pistol, dumping every bullet he had into the cop. As Jonny and the cop lay there, dead, the two boys fled.

Angelo is upset by the fact that he had just killed a cop. He knew that he was just trying to do his job and probably had a family, but innocents are a common casualty within vendettas. Angelo just kept picturing Yano bleeding from his wound on his back when the cop shot him. He couldn't see that same fate brought down on Gino. He did what needed to be done. As the two boys fled the scene, Angelo looks at Gino,

"Let's go find his friend."

Angelo and Gino drive through Jonny's neighborhood for hours looking for this guy with no luck.

"Let's just park where we met them last time and see what happens."

The two sit there for almost an hour and began growing impatient.

"Do you think he could've heard about Jonny already," Gino asks.

"I hope not, or he could be anywhere right now. He could assume that it was us, and if he did, well he'd be stupid to hang around."

"There are probably a few other guys out there that would like to clip Jonny though, I don't think he would just assume it were us right away."

"let's just go back and call the number I got, maybe we'll get lucky."

Sure enough, the phone number that they had did not go to only Jonny, but to a warehouse where the guys hung out at. Gino began talking to the friend and let him know that they need another shipment. The guy was excited to hear from them and didn't seem as if he had heard about his friend Jonny's demise yet. He told Gino that he would meet up with them in about an hour.

"Should we come up with a plan? What do you want to do? How should we handle this?"

"Gino, calm down. I have already taken care of it. All you need to do is follow my instructions."

The Return

AS GINO PACES back and forth awaiting the shipment, he just keeps thinking about what Angelo told him. Gino is holding a handful of little rocks, tossing them one by one at the sidewalk as if one were trying to skip them across the water. As the guy pulls up, Gino is to toss the rest of the pebbles at a nearby dumpster. This would be the signal for Angelo to jump out and open fire.

As the man pulls up, he sees Gino casual standing there skipping stones. The guy pulls into a parking spot and gets out of the car.

"How you doing tonight?" the guy asked Gino.

Gino tossed the rocks at the dumpster, but right then he noticed Angelo standing across the street.

'What the hell,' he thought. Just then Gino heard a rustling inside the dumpster. Gino was confused. What did Angelo just do? Did he set up Gino? Gino and the delivery guy both looked at the dumpster. Gino took a few steps backward, nervous. The dumpster lid flew open and bullets started flying. Gino quickly jumped behind a parked car unaware of what the hell was happening. The victim's face quickly changed from confused to scared and then to hurt as the bullets tore through his flesh. He fell to the ground twitching and screaming in agony. The gunman walked up to him as he desperately grasped for one last breath, the blood leaking into his throat drowning him. The holes in his lungs were preventing the air from entering as the oxygen he so badly fought for. Suddenly, one more gunshot rang out and the air stood silent. As the gunshots quieted down Gino pops his head up. It takes him a moment but he suddenly realizes that it is Vinnie standing where Angelo was supposed to be. Gino jumps up and rushes over to him.

"Holy fuckin' shit man am I glad to see you!"

As Vinnie hops from the dumpster Gino hugs him.

"How's your leg?"

"It's good."

How have you been? Hows my sister? How the hell…what the hell are you doing here?"

Angelo walks back across the street laughing. He explains that he set this up as a surprise but there's no time to talk about now. They have some cleaning to do. As Gino and Angelo pick up the bloody corpse and carry him to the trunk of their car, Vinnie hooks up the hose and begins to spray the blood away.

"Damn, I missed this," Vinnie says while laughing.

The gang drove the body down to Jonny's neighborhood and tossed him over that bridge that they saw earlier. The body bounced off of large rocks as the current pulled it downstream. As the guys are laughing and catching up with Vinnie, having a great time, Yano lays on his skinny mattress upon a metal bed. He thinks about the mess hall massacre. It's been a month since all of that had happened and its time to plot his next attack. The rats that had been telling on Yano, the Warden, something has to happen now. Things inside the prison have quieted down so this was the perfect time to hit. The Italians and what was left of the Nation were no longer fighting, mainly because the Nation had less than a fist full of members left. The Irish were quietly taking over certain businesses that Yano promised them. Nobody is expecting anything.

Yano knows that once something happens to the Warden's little friends they will automatically assume it was him. He had to find a place to hide the bodies. Just then Yano had an idea, maybe his craziest idea yet.

Rocco is walking down the corridor and sees Vito. He stops and tells him that Bruno is looking for him.

"What does he want?"

"I'm not sure but he seemed excited, he says he has something important to tell you. I think he went downstairs."

Vito hurries and finishes what he is doing so he can meet up with Bruno. Meanwhile, Bruno is being told the same thing by another one of Yano's soldiers. As Bruno enters the room in the basement he meets up with Vinnie. Before either of them can say anything a loud noise fills the air as the door slams shut. The two, startled look back and see Yano and Antonio standing there. Yano quickly swings a metal pipe and hits Vito in the head, knocking him unconscious. Antonio swings his pipe and crashes Bruno's knee, snapping his leg. As Bruno falls to the floor, Antonio proceeds to beat him to death. Yano wants Vito alive to feel the pain, even if it were only for a moment. The two began to go to work on the bodies, cutting them into pieces with knives given to them by the Irish guy who worked in the kitchen.

As the two are dismembering the bodies, Rocco is heading to the Warden's office.

"Hey, I just saw Vito and Bruno head downstairs."

"What? Nobody is allowed down there."

"I don't know, but I also saw Yano follow them."

The Warden jumps from his chair. He figured that Yano must have found out that the two were snitches for the Warden. He was finally going to catch Yano red-handed. As the Warden ran downstairs, he kicks open the basement door. He expected to find Yano, but there were only the pieces of his most trusted informants. What happened next was completely unexpected, to the Warden and every guard and inmate as well. The Warden walked into the room and saw the two bodies leaned up against the wall. Legs cut off, arms torn from the torso, and both bearing Sicilian bow ties. This was a message. The necks were slit and the tongues of each snitch were pulled from the mouth and out of the throat. The Warden became sick. He turned and violently began to vomit.

As the Warden's lunch makes its second appearance of the day, Antonio appears from behind the shadows and tosses a large bucket of cleaning liquids on the Warden. As the Warden looks at Anotnio, confused, Yano approaches from the shadows. Yano smiles, lights a match, and tosses it. The Warden quickly goes up in flames, burning and screaming. He runs at Yano and Antonio but they jump from the flaming path. The Warden falls to the floor and rolls around violently. Yano turns and exits the room. Antonio follows, shuts the door, and quickly runs upstairs.

The Warden's body lay there on the floor, burnt, next to the two chopped up snitches. Yano thinks that he will not be getting paroled after his last few months, but also knows that the Warden would not have kept his word and put in a good word for him. Not after the mess hall incident. He has just got to take his chances by himself at this point. He figures that if the Warden isn't there to say anything good about Yano, he also isn't there to say anything bad. So Yano has a fifty-fifty chance now. He thinks he has better odds without the Warden there. The two murderers walk back to their cells talking about what's for lunch, completely unphased by what they had just done.

It only takes a day or two before all of the guards start to talk. They all notice that the Warden has not been in. At Gino's next visit with Yano, he also hears what of the Warden's disappearing act. Gino now knows that he has to get Yano out. He has to consider Tommy's plan.

The same day, the police show up at the prison to question some of the guards. The Warden's wife had reported him missing. None of the guards knew what happened, so none of them had anything valuable to tell the police. The police ask if the Warden has any enemies who are capable of making him disappear like this. The guards all mention Yano, and the remaining members of the Nation.

Yano acts surprised by the news as the cops tell him.

"Yeah, I hated the Warden, but what inmate in here doesn't?"

Yano deliberately points out that he is locked in a cage most of the day, only being able to come out for chow and showers.

"How the hell would anybody pull off something like that? Look at how many guards are walking around at any given time. A hit on the Warden, in this place, would not go unnoticed for long."

The police begin to walk around the prison more and search the place for clues. As they head down to the basement, one guard yells out,

"There's no point going in there. That doors always locked and the inmates don't have keys."

The two cops take his word for it and conclude that whatever happened to the Warden happened outside of the prison walls. As they walk back up the stairs, Rocco is watching from an upper tier. He lets out a sigh of relief and tells Yano that they are in the clear.

Tommy

POW! POW! POW! Gunshots explode through the air as Tommy ran around the corner. Three Black Hand members running behind him. The chase began when Tommy confronted one man for harassing an elderly woman. The little old lady told the men that her fruit stand didn't make enough money to pay her dues for the month, he got angry. Tommy looked over just in time to see the man push the elderly lady to the ground. As the man pulled his pistol to shoot the woman, Tommy jumped him from behind. He began to beat the man as two more men ran up from the side of him. The chase started and gunshots followed.

Tommy ran through yards, jumping fences, and dodging hedges. The men relentlessly pursued Tommy and finally caught him right in front of Angelo's home. The men began to beat Tommy until his body fell limp. Angelo heard the screams and ran outside. He saw the men beating on Tommy and he pulled his pistol. Angelo could've just backed back up into the house and let the members handle Tommy, but Angelo hated the Black Hand with a passion and couldn't pass up this opportunity. Angelo pulled his trigger and put two bullets in the back of one man's head. The second man turned and grappled with Angelo, fighting for the gun. As the two roll around on the ground, Angelo begins to lose his grip on the gun. He quickly pulls the trigger and lets loose two more bullets into this guy's chest.

Angelo rolls the man off of him just as the third man is getting near. He always has his gun drawn and opens fire on Angelo. Angelo returns fire and drops the man in his steps. Before Angelo ran back into the house he saw his chance. He let his last bullet fly. Hot lead buried its way into Tommy's skull. He then fled back into the house as he heard the screeching tires of police cars coming around the corner. Angelo quickly calls Gino and tells him that they need to meet up and talk. Gino drove over to pick up Angelo and saw all of the cop cars. Angelo was down the street waiving for Gino. He hopped in the car and quickly explained what was going on. As they drive away, Angelo notices the police walking up to his door.

"They know! They know it was me! I just killed four people, I'm going away forever!"

Gino needed to find out what the cops knew, he pulled over a few blocks away and walked back towards Angelo's house. He walked up to a neighbor's house and asked what was going on.

"Your friend, Angelo, he killed a bunch of guys."

"Do the cops know it was him?"

"No. I think I'm the only person who witnessed it and I didn't say anything. They are just canvassing the neighborhood in hopes of finding out what happened."

"Well, just remember to keep your mouth shut."

"Hey, I love what you guys did a few years ago, and I want you to do it again. I'm not saying shit. You can trust me."

Gino nods at the guy and walks off. He walked back to the car and Let Angelo know that the cops didn't know anything. Angelo was relieved but still nervous. What the old man lied to Gino and was going to tell the cops. Angelo hated the idea of killing an old man but hated the idea of going to prison even more.

"How do you know he didn't say anything?"

"Because I saw the look in his eyes. He was upset at the fact that I even had to tell him to keep his mouth shut."

"You're sure about this?"

"Definitely. He seemed relieved to see those thugs laying in a pool of their blood. Trust me, he isn't going to talk."

Angelo feels even more at ease when he sees the trust Gino has for the old man.

"I don't know if I believe him or not, but I trust you, and I trust your judgment. I think that I should go home now and get the cops away from my mom's house. I don't want it to appear as if I'm hiding from them."

Gino is hesitant at this idea, but it sounds smart. Angelo didn't do anything if it didn't make sense so Gino drove him back home.

"Just be careful what you say. Keep it short, keep it simple. You need to keep your story easy to remember, in case they come back later the details don't change. Getting caught in a lie would be very bad."

As Angelo walked back up to his house, one officer stopped him. "Did you see what happened here?"

"No, I didn't see anything. I was inside eating. I heard a few shots and some screams and that was it."

"Why did you run? Where are you coming from?"

"I didn't run. I went down the street to speak with a friend. I then came back because I have nothing to hide. I didn't see what happened. All I know is that when I exited my house, I saw people lying in blood."

When the police finally vacated the area, Angelo went to speak with his neighbor. He had to thank him for not talking.

"This is our neighborhood," the old man began. "We built this, and it belongs to us. If it weren't for us these damn punks would be living in boxes. Remove them, give the neighborhood back to us. Nobody around here is going to stop you or get your way. We all know it was you and your friends and there is a reason that nobody has said anything."

"I'm glad to hear you say that."

"Hopefully you rid them for good this time. It was so peaceful for those couple of years. I have nothing but respect for you young men."

Turning Up The Heat

BACK INSIDE THE prison walls, things are starting to heat up. The guards all knew that whatever happened to the Warden happened within these walls. He only lives a few blocks away, so as he walks home he is either close enough for the guards in the tower to see him, or close enough for his wife, kids, and neighbors to see. Getting to him on his walk home would be almost impossible without anyone noticing. There's not much of a middle ground. No, they know that something happened to him at work, they just don't know what.

His disappearance happened in the middle of his shift and he is not the type to abandon his post. They are to busy to conduct a complete lockdown and search of the facility, but they have to try. It's going to take days but they owe it to the Warden to get to the bottom of this. Guards began taking turns coming in early and staying late so they could search every area. Some even skipped lunch breaks. Yano started getting nervous as he noticed the guards becoming more vigilant about the search. It was the first time that he started to second guess one of his decisions.

Pauli comes in and tries to tell Yano to stop doubting himself. Even if the Warden is found, there is no evidence pointing to him. It's going to take a little while but eventually, the bodies will be discovered. Will they be able to tell who these bodies belong to? Their identities cannot remain unknown forever. As the guards continue searching, they come very close to the room in the basement multiple times but each time they seem to skip over it. Its as if they either know he's in there and does not really want to find him, or they truly believe that there is no way that any inmates could've gotten into that particular room. Either way, it is nerve-wracking for Yano the entire tie. Days go by and the search does not seem to quiet down. These guys are relentless and determined. The bodies will be discovered, it's just a matter of time. Eventually, federal agents are going to be brought in. There is no doubt in Yano's mind that this move guaranteed his chances of not getting parole. Not just losing parole, but having additional time added on. Yano knows he cannot do another ten years. How can he get past this? Is there anything that he can do? It might just be up to Gino and Angelo at this point to secure Yano's release.

"Little Italy is under attack. Under attack by violent, extortionists. By pistol-toting thugs who are willing to use them for any reason. The streets are quickly filling with blood because of these vultures. Some of the neighborhood's residents have taken it upon themselves to become vigilantes. They think it is the only solution to this problem, but I assure you, it is not. We, the police, are not ignoring this situation. We are trying our best to bring these extortionists as well as the vigilantes to justice. Even vigilante murder is wrong. Some of you believe otherwise, but let me tell you this. The streets run red with the blood of your children, your parents, your siblings, and it is because you choose not to give the proper information to the authorities."

The police walk the entire neighborhood giving speeches and trying to convince the residents to come forward.

"Unless you come forward and help us, there is nothing that we can do."

Eventually, the police presence began to twindle back to almost none. The neighborhood had fallen back into the hands of the corrupt. Police cannot help if nobody helps them. People seemed almost more afraid of them than of the Black Hand. Nobody left their homes while the police presence remained strong. Everybody went into hiding, including Gino, Vinnie, and Angelo. The police noticed that the crime rate dropped tremendously during this month-long patrol of the neighborhood and decided to call it a job well done. The truly thought that maybe they had made a difference, where in reality, the violence was just on pause.

The very first day that the police left the neighborhood, the Black Hand reacted. They had to retaliate for Angelo's murdering of three members. Later that morning the sirens of the fire truck screeching through the neighborhood as it stopped in front of a house. The Hand had no idea who killed their men so they took it upon themselves to react with haste, burning down random homes. The house that was caught on fire was that of a single mother with three children of her own. The husband had been a victim of street violence a few short years previously. The mother was tied to the bed and beaten. Her legs were broken. The children were left locked in a closet with no chance of escape. Gino, Vinnie, and Angelo all stood in the crowd of neighbors as the fire department brought out body bag after body bag.

Angelo fell to his knees and broke into tears, knowing that this happened because of his actions. These kids and their mother were innocent, yet somehow, Angelo had condemned them to death.

"Let's go! I'm ready to start this damn war right fuckin now!" Angelo exclaimed.

"I don't care if you guys are ready or not, I'm not waiting for Yan anymore. This shit has to happen now before anybody else is hurt because of us."

"Ang, I know you're hurting right now, but we have to be smart about this."

Gino chimed in, "We need to get Yano out of prison today! We can't wait five more months. This shit has to end, now"

"Those mother fuckers killed little kids Gino! Fuck your brother, we have to react tonight!"

"Hey! You think I want to continue waiting? These guys killed my dad and my mom. I want them all to burn as bad as you do, but we have to be smart. We cannot let our emotions run wild."

It all makes sense to Angelo, but he does not want to see reason. He only wants to see the blood spill.

"Before Tommy died he gave me the name of the guy who runs the parole board meetings. We can go tonight and get to him. We can have Yano out by the end of the week."

Angelo nods as Gino talks, not paying attention. All he can see in his mind is the body bags being brought out of the burnt home that was once filled with the laughter of three little children. Vinnie doesn't agree with Gino.

"Fuck this! Something has to happen."

Vinnie storms off and heads back to his house. He goes inside and grabs his gun, a little six-shooter with a couple of extra bullets in hand. He fills his pockets with the pistol and ammo and heads back out into the darkness. Vinnie heads back to the warehouse to get the guys on his side. As he walks back in, Gino notices the handle of his gun sticking out of his pocket.

"What's the gun for Vinnie?"

"Protection. These streets ain't safe anymore."

Vinnie pulls the shirt down concealing the handle of the weapon.

"Don't go do anything stupid, Vinnie! I know you don't agree with what we say but it's the smart move. You don't want to go back to prison, do you? Or die? We cannot afford to lose you and we don't want to lose another friend."

Vinnie doesn't care about what they say, he wants vengeance now. He doesn't listen at all, he simply turns and walks out of the building. Vinnie begins to think of Gino as a coward. He was always the one rushing to get this done while he and Angelo had to be the voice of reason. Now that the two of them are ready to go, Gino seems as if he is scared. Vinnie walks the streets for over an hour and finds himself in front of a house. This is a house belonging to a Black Hand member used as a safe house. Vinnie knows that there are probably multiple targets in this house right now. Vinnie stares at the house wondering. Is Gino right or should he follow his heart? Gino has never steered him wrong, yet neither has his heart.

Finally, Vinnie said fuck it and hopped the fence. As his feet hit the grass, he heard voices. A few large guys were heading his way, walking off of the porch. Vinnie jumped behind a bush and waited for them to pass. As they pass, Vinnie sneaks out and runs down the shadow by the fence. He is in a perfect spot, but there is no way out. He has inadvertently cornered himself in the yard. Gino was right, there is safety in numbers, but it's too late now. He has to keep going, he looks around and sees an upper window that is easily accessible. As he begins to climb the tree the guards walk by again. He stops, stays perfectly still, and then moves towards the window again as they pass.

As Vinnie gets to the window he sees multiple people standing in the room. He waits for two of them to exit. He then jumps from the tree, into the window. As he crashed through the glass and rolled on the floor, he jumped to his feet and began shooting. Vinnie easily takes out the two men in the room, but the shots alert everyone and men begin to run upstairs to investigate. Vinnie scurries to hide behind a desk as more men enter the room. As their gunfight begins, another man is climbing the tree in which Vinnie had moments before been sitting in. As he approached the window, he was on the right side of the room to see Vinnie hiding behind the desk. He pulled his weapon and fired, hitting Vinnie in the shoulder. Vinnie turns and shoots the man, knocking him out of the tree.

Vinnie stands and continues to fire shots at the doorway where the men are coming from. As he gets back by the window, his pistol runs dry. He jumps from the room back to the tree. As he is in mid-air, three bullets are fired off. Two find homes in Vinnie's leg and the third in the tree. Vinnie falls from the tree and immediately rises and tries to exit the yard. As he jumps the fence, another bullet finds a home in Vinnie's back. Vinnie fell to the ground on the other side of the fence. Full of adrenaline, Vinnie can pull himself to his feet and limp away quickly.

"Have you seen Vinnie?" gino asked Angelo.

"Yeah, I saw him last night. He said he was going for a walk."

"I can't seem to find him anywhere, he's not at his house."

"Well shit, I hope he didn't do anything stupid."

"What do you mean?"

"Last night when I saw him, he had a gun with him. He said it was just for protection and I believed him."

"Well fuck! The entire neighborhood is buzzing about some gunshots they heard last night. It had to be him!"

"I didn't hear anything."

"Neither did I but I went to bed early. Start calling hospitals looking for him."

Angelo reached for the phone and started to dial the number to the local hospital.

"I know how he feels. It's just like when they killed my parents, but if he doesn't listen to us, he's going to get himself killed."

Angelo got a hold of someone at the hospital who says that a young man, nameless, was brought into the hospital the previous night with multiple gunshot wounds. A passing car saw him laying on the side of the road and pulled over to help him.

"It's got to be him, right?"

Angelo nods, "Let's go see him. We need to find out what the fuck happened and what we can expect to happen next."

The two head to the hospital and speak with Vinnie. He tells them both exactly how he went off half-cocked and killed a few guys. He says that he dropped at least three of them before barely escaping with his life.

"Some car was driving by and I was able to wave hi down. He got out and recognized me. He must know me from the neighborhood, but he says that the neighborhood needs me and I need to get fixed. So he tossed my body into the backseat of his car and drove me here."

Gino told Angelo to sit with Vinnie for a while and keep an eye out, just in case anyone else found out where he was and came looking for trouble.

"What are you going to do?"

"Get my brother out of prison!"

Desperate Times

GINO TAKES THE name and address that Tommy gave him. He heads to that address. He sees a man, standing in the front yard. Gino peaks at him from behind a tree. He also sees a young boy, maybe five years old. His wife, sitting on the stairs. They seem to be having a pretty good day. They live in a neighborhood that has no worries of Black Hand organizations. They live in a neighborhood with no gunshots and bloodshed. They know not of what Gino knows. This guy, he s in charge of judging the inmates. It is his jb t decide whether they deserve to leave prison, but he cannot even relate to any of what the guys have been through to get put in there. How can you possibly judge a man that you cannot relate too?

How can this man decide who is well enough to leave, and to come back to the same environment that got him locked up anyway? It seems too unreal to Gino. This man, his wife, they have no idea what it's like for people like the Scarpacci family. Gino sits and watches the family, contemplating his next move. He has no plan. He decided to wing it. Gino popped out from behind the tree and started toward the family. The man looked up and saw Gino, he quickly told his wife to take the child inside. Gino walks up and starts an innocent conversation.

"Hey, how are you doing today?"

"I'm doing ok. How 'bout yourself?"

"Oh, I've been better."

"Do I know you?"

"Nope. We have not been formally introduced."

"Well, can I help you with something?"

"You sure can. My brother, Yano Scarpacci, he's up for parole in a few months. You're going to grant it."

"I'll grant it if I feel he deserves it, and I can tell you right now that I know for a fact he doesn't. He is a suspect in almost two hundred murders inside of those prison walls."

"He deserves it. Nobody deserves it more than he does."

"I'm sorry son, I truly believe that your brother will never see the light of day again beyond those walls."

"I believe that he will. I also believe that you're going to make sure of it, and I also believe that it's going to happen by the end of the week, not months from now."

"Well, I have no control over when parole dates are set. Even if I wanted to let him out, he has to wait until his meeting, which I believe is still four months away."

"No. He'll be out by the end of the week. I appreciate your cooperation."

As the man begins to talk some more, Gino turns and heads back across the street. The man yelling from behind.

"I don't know who the hell you think you are, but you can't scare me!"

The man wakes a few hours later. Lying in his bed he thinks of what Gino said to him. He knows Yano, he knows Yano all too well. Why was Gino so nice? He didn't threaten him or anything. He just assumed that he would go along with this. There was no bribe either. What was Gino's end game? The man rolls over and sees his wife, asleep. He rises from bed and heads to the bathroom. As he flushes he hears a car drive by. 'Why did that sound so loud,' he thought. He headed down the hall only to notice the window was opened. As he turned to run he scurried to his son's room. He was still lying there, asleep. Next to his bed, on the table sat a single bullet. Standing on end, sending a quiet message. How did Gino get in without being heard? Al he could think now was that his son could be dead and there's not one thing he could've done to stop it. Gino is stealthy. Is this type of thing worth it? Should he let Yano go? No, he says to himself. He is not going to be intimidated by anybody. He just needs to add an extra measure of security now. He has to protect his family.

The next day, the man and his son are outside playing. The man looks up and sees Gino down the street resting in the shade of a big oak tree. The man sends his son inside and marches over to Gino.

"How are you today, sir?" Gino started.

"If you ever come close to my son again, I'll… I'll… well, I'll kill you myself."

"Whatever do you mean?" Gino smirked and taunted the man.

"You didn't even budge when your son was in danger last night, what makes you think you could do anything to prevent anything? Are you going to stay awake all night? Every night?"

"If that's what it takes, yes!"

"Then I'll hit during the day. Are you going to have cops sitting in front of your house?"

"I have connections, yes! I can have multiple cruisers here all night."

"Well, then I'll come in the back. You see, no matter what precautions you take, I'm a step in front of you. This is not my first day of this lifestyle. It doesn't matter how good your eyesight is, or becomes, you cant see every inch of the shadows, and that's where I'll be. Waiting patiently."

"You need to leave my family alone! I swear to Christ I'll bury you!"

"Release Yano, by the end of the week and your kid has nothing to fear."

Gino turns to walk away and the man whimpers a few last words, something about not being scared of Gino or Yano.

As the end of the week rolls around, Yano is still in prison. The man doesn't give in to Gino. As he arrived home from work, he steps from his car. He shuts the door and approaches his home, looking all around for Gino but sees nothing. He puts his key inside the lock and turns gently. The door swings open. The man peeks in and lets out a sigh of relief. Nothing seems to be out of the ordinary, but why is it so quiet? His son can usually be heard playing from the other room or running to greet him at the door as he returned home from work. Today the house stood silent.

As he walks into the house he notices something. A large kitchen knife stabbed into the living room wall. He begins to run through the house and yell for his wife and child, but there are no responses. He reaches his bedroom and sees his wife. She laid silently on the bed, throat slit, and body bled dry. There was so much blood on the floor and the sheets that there couldn't have been anyway a single drop of blood remained inside of her body. He instantly dropped to his knees, clutching her tight and screaming. His entire life just flipped upside down. He then thought about his son. He rose to his feet and ran to the boy's bedroom. There was nobody. No blood. No knives stabbed in the wall. Just an empty room and an open window. The man fell to his knees and once again started screaming, crying, yelling. His wife was dead and his son, missing. As he looked up he saw a note on the table. He opened it up and saw the words, 'free him.'

That very moment the man ran back to work and started the paperwork to get Yano's parole hearing moved up. The police were not allowing it to happen because, despite the fact that no body was yet found, Yano was still a suspect. The man did everything he could, but the police responded the same. The next day the man arrived at work and demanded that either Yano be charged with something or allowed his right to parole. The guards and the police couldn't do anything about it. It was the law, Yano had this right, and they couldn't charge him with murder if there was no corpse. Yano was granted his parole hearing and immediately released from prison.

Homecoming

A S YANO WALKS out of the prison gate he feels confused. It has been a long time since he has been on this side of the wall and he isn't quite sure how to feel or what to do. He always thought that once he was out, he would be welcomed with open, loving arms from his mom and sister. Neither of which are there. It is finally hitting Yano how different life is now. Gino stands there by the car, smiling. He is excited to have his brother back. As Yano gets close, they hug. Yano looks at him and smiles.

"Let's go home."

As they drive away, Yano stares at the prison in his side-view mirror. It's all in the past now. Time to focus on the present, learning to live outside the walls again. Gino tries to talk to Yano the entire drive home, but Yano doesn't pay attention. All he thinks about is finding Arabella. He has missed her so much over the years and the thought of her always warmed his body. He dreamed of the day he could see her again for many years and now that dream seems to be a possibility.

"Have you heard from Arabella recently?"

"Shit, not for a long time. After Talapini's house burned down, I saw her maybe twice. It was as if her family got scared and moved to a different neighborhood as soon as Talapini left."

"You say that Talapini left like he moved and didn't die. Why?"

"Well, his body was never found. Even with the ones that were burnt, his death was never confirmed. We assume he died since we never heard from or about him again, but I'm not sure really."

"So, these new guys. Who are they?"

"A lot of them used to run with Talapini. We think that after he left, a new boss took over and began to rebuild."

"So it's the same organization? The Black Hand?"

"That's what we think.

The brothers pull up to the warehouse and exit the vehicle. Yano stands and stares at the building.

"I planned to have a good crew out here by the time I got out. With Dino dead, Vinnie hiding out, Tommy and Carlo dead, its just the three of us. Definitely not how I wanted to come back."

"There are more guys that have come to see me over the years though, Yano."

"Yeah, I sent a bunch of guys to see you. Where are they all?"

"I told them wed be in contact and to stay close. Most of them live in the neighborhood north of us."

Gino puts his arm around Yano and walks him into the building. Everyone jumps out from behind furniture and yells surprise. As Yano's body goes into a quick shock and he jumps backward, he noticed a lot of people he hasn't seen in a while. Guys that were paroled years ago, guys who were loyal to Yano in the fight against the Nation. Yano looks through everyone and sees Vinnie. He instantly smiles and heads over to talk to him.

"How's life, Vinnie?"

"Oh you know, I can't complain."

"The leg?"

"Good as new."

"And my sister?"

"She's good. She's staying with my mom, helping her out around the house. She's very happy there Yano. She has a lot of friends, a boyfriend who is a good guy, just living a normal life away from all of this."

Yano is relieved to hear that Rosaria is doing so well. He turns to look around again and is disappointed, Arabella is not there. The nights that Yano spent in prison, lonely, he would think of her. He always dreamed of the day he could once again be in her arms. As he looked around and found her face nowhere, he thought, maybe its time to let her go. As the party continued, loud noises rang from outside, though Yano and his guests couldn't hear due to the loud noises inside. The next morning though, the results of the previous night's conflict would be known to all.

The smell of burnt lumber reeks through the neighborhood. Smoke still filling the air. Yano comes outside, has a good morning stretch, and notices the noise. The noise of people crying. He sees the smoke. He knows something terrible has happened. He walks down the stairs and down the street. As he gets to the end of the block he turns left. He cannot believe his eyes. Three major stores have been burnt down. Yano walks closer to ask what has happened. The neighbors cry and Yano can barely make out what they are saying. Through the ears and the screams, he hears that somebody died.

"Mr. Marino, the grocer. He and his wife were inside when it burned."

"That's not all," another started. "The girl who owned the store next door was also in there, with her daughter of sixteen."

Yano stood there and listened to the people and heard tht a total of seven people had been killed in this accident. Yano knows it was no accident though. He turns to the elderly man next to him and asks how the fire started.

"You know God damn well how it started! They did it! These people couldn't afford to make their payment, so they were burnt alive. The fire just got out of control and spread to the two neighboring buildings. This is terrible! Something must be done about this!"

People cry, they want justice, but every one of them knows that they cannot go to the police. This has to be a vigilante-style. Their neighborhood heroes had to hear the pleading. It was their only hope.

"Eliminate these scum!"

"Once and for all!"

"For good this time!"

Everyone was yelling, almost chanting together. They all knew who Yano was and what he had done in his past. They wanted him to hear them and they hope that he will listen. Yano heads back to the warehouse and wakes everybody up.

"Its time to finish this."

"Finish what?" Angelo asked.

"Did we even start anything yet?" Gino giggled.

"Get up! You know exactly what it is that I am talking about! Its time we go to war!"

All the guys are now awake. They're all wide-eyed and ready. People died and the only way to fix this is for more people to die so that even more people do not die. It's a confusing life to live, but they all understand it.

"One of the victims is alive. He's in the hospital right now. Vinnie, you go with Gino to visit and see how he is doing."

Gino and Vinnie head down the street to St. Mary Magdeline's hospital. They make their way in and eventually find the guy's room. As they are about to walk in, Vinnie glances to his left. A big burly guy is also walking towards the room, knife in hand. He must've come to quiet the survivor. Vinnie hollers at the man and quickly runs towards him. As Gino follows, the big man turns to run. The boys follow him down the hall, jumping and dodging the obstacles the man tries to make. He bursts through a door and proceeds down the large staircase. They were on the fourth level, so there were many stairs to run down. As the man turns to go down the next set of stairs, there was a box on the wall, he opens the door and Vinnie runs into it. As Vinnie tumbles, Gino notices that there is an ax in this box. It is a just in case firebox with the ax and a fire hose.

Gino grabs the ax and jumps down the next few stairs. He runs down a few more and jumps down the last few. He does this multiple times before finally catching up with the man. One quick swing and the ax is placed in its new home. The blood starts pooling from the massive slit in between the man's shoulder blades. As he falls to the ground, Gino pulls him to his knees. At this point, Vinnie finally catches back up and helps lift the man. They both go back and forth questioning him.

"Who is your boss?"

"Where can we find him?"

"Who gave the order to come silence this man?"

"Who do you work for?"

The man has no response. A simple smile graces his face as he slowly slips from this world. His body falls limp and slumps forward, face-first into the tile floor. Gino and Vinnie knew that questioning him was pointless. These were men of honor, scum bags, but loyal to the core. He was never going to say anything to them. Answering questions is worse than death in their life. The punishment for breaking their oath was that of a pain far worse than death. The two sneak out the exit and make their way back to the warehouse. The man they were sent to see is safe, for now.

The Information

THE TWO RETURNED to the warehouse and told Yano and Angelo what had happened.

"We left his dead ass sitting in the staircase at the hospital."

"How ironic is that? Injured while in the hospital and the doctors can't even save you."

As Gino and Vinnie laughed about their recent excitement, Yano barked at them.

"Shut up! Do you think this is funny? Is this really a good time for laughter?" No! This is a sad time, innocent people just lost their lives last night. Laughter should be the last thing I hear right now!"

Yano gives a big speech about respect and the fact that this couple was murdered for the simple fact that they didn't earn enough money. The speech then goes on to how pitiful these guys are, how heartless, how badly in need of a death sentence. Yano sits down with Angelo to devise a plan. Gino and Vinnie, feeling like their fun was just ruined like a father yelling at his kids for running in the house, went outside.

"That was a bunch of bull shit," Gino says.

"There ain't no reason for him to go off on us like that."

"I don't know, Gino. I can kind of understand his point. This is a pretty fucked up time. Even though we may have fun living this lifestyle, a lot of people are actually suffering."

The two stand outside and talk until the sun begins to set. Not long after the sun decided to go down, the Black Hand decided to get up. Two guys start walking down the street. They turn the opposite way of the boys. Neither of them says anything, they simply look at each other and they know. They know what each other is thinking. They know what they have to do. They run down the street, grabbing a large branch that lay on the sidewalk. As they get closer Gino smashes the branch over one of the guy's heads. As he falls, the second man turns towards his assailants. Vinnie jumps and lands a swift punch to the bridge of his nose. Both guys fall unconscious.

Vinnie runs back up the street to grab Yano and Angelo.

"Are you fucking' stupid?"

Yano usually refrains from the foul language as he thinks it makes him sound uneducated, however, when he does swear, you know he is extremely upset.

"This is not the time to go half-cocked attacking people!"

"Yano, this could be a good thing," Angelo reassures him.

"How?"

"Interrogation? You want to end this? Lets fuckin' find out what we need to know and end this, tonight!"

All three of them run back down towards Gino and carry the men back to the warehouse. As Vinnie finishes tieing the second man up, the first man begins to wake.

"What the hell?"

"Shut up! I'm going to say this one time. Scream, and I'll kill you right here. Be cooperative, and well, who knows."

Yano gives false assurances to try and make the man feel a little safer.

"What do you want from me? I will tell you nothing!"

The man spits on the floor, at Yano's feet. Yano knows that this isn't going to be easy. It is going to take some morbid stuff to break these men. Just then, the second guy becomes aware of the situation. He seems a little less scary. He looks around the room, eyeballing each of them, nervously. He opens his mouth as if to say something, then instantly shuts his mouth.

"What is it? You have something to tell us?"

The man shakes his head no. He is more afraid of his partner than the guys holding them hostage.

"Who is your boss and where can we find him?"

The first man laughs as the second man's eyes swell. Yano can see what is to happen next. He says no more words, reaches under his shirt and grabs the gun by the handle. The pistol comes out at an angle that leads the barrel towards the man's forehead.

"What? Are you going to shoot me? If you do you'll never…"

BOOM! Yano pulls his trigger and stops the man's sentence short by a minimum of five words. The second man starts to cry. How did he ever become a part of this gruesome, violent, organization with such weak nerves?

"Now, do you have anything to tell us?"

"Everything! Anything! Yes! I will tell you anything you want to know."

"You're Black Hand?"

"Yes."

"The same organization that Don TAlapini lead?"

"Yes."

"Who is the new boss?"

"Wh… wh… what do you mean the *new* boss?"

"Talapini, we killed him. Who took over?"

"Talapini isn't dead."

"What do you mean? How is that possible? We burned his house down on top of him, I saw it happen!"

"He escaped through the back door."

"Bull shit!"

Yano hits the man with the butt of the pistol.

"I swear to you, Talapini is alive."

As the hostage begins to cry, the brothers look at each other, then towards Angelo.

"Could that be possible?"

"It would explain why his body was never found."

Yano can't believe this, but Talapini coming back and reviving the Black Hand does make more sense than a new boss emerging. A new boss couldn't possibly run this organization as ruthless as Talapini, could he? No this has to be Don Talapini, but how did he escape? Yano tried to think back, didn't they have every exit covered? It was a long time ago so it was hard to remember but he was almost positive that they did. Maybe as the ran from the police. Maybe as Yano's body was filling with lead, Talapini was escaping.

"Where is he?"

"The big house, top of the hill, Vinton street, right off of sixteenth. You can't miss it."

Yano had the perfect punishment for this man, for all of the men that they were after. Death by fire, as so many of their victims died, including his mother. Yano nods at Angelo and looks toward the door. Angelo looks over to see what Yano was looking at. He sees the gas tank and immediately understands. He walks over and grabs the tank, walks back, and begins to pour. The man started screaming even louder as he realized what was happening. Yano, Vinnie, and Gino turned to exit the warehouse as Angelo struck and tossed the match. As the four of them walked out, a loud screaming echoed through the warehouse. The wall in front of them shined orange from the reflection of the flames.

The Final Act

T HE DAY HAS finally come. Don Talapini and the Black Hand die tonight. Yano stares at himself in the mirror as the rest of the guys load up the weapons. The four of them pus six other guys from Yano's prison crew. Much more power than they had the first attempt at Talapini's life and the first attempt was pretty damn close. Yano walks out of the bathroom and looks at the guys.

"Either we all come back, or none of us do. Nobody goes to jail this time around. If the police show up, we kill them too. Everybody fights till their last breath, nobody leaves while even one man is still left on Talapini's property."

The men exit the warehouse and walk toward the cars. As they load up, Gino turns and looks back. Not in any way thinking it is the last time that he'll be there, but just thinking of how far they've come and how long they have all been waiting for this day. Yano puts a hand on his shoulder, and Gino turns back to look at him. They both smile at each other and get into the car. The gang drives down the street and into another neighborhood. No wonder they thought Talpini was dead. He left the neighborhood and stayed indoors, hardly anybody seeing him.

It took almost a half an hour to reach the big hill in which Talapini lived on top of. As they drove up the street, Gino glances out the window and sees a street sign, '16th st.' it says. He now knows that they are getting close. They drive a little more and hit a stop sign. He looks out the window again, and again sees a sign, 'Vinton St.' They're close. They see the hill and the house on top. It is a blue house with grey shingles. Two-story with a huge yard. There is also a fence, well, not so much a fence but a wall. A brick wall about eight feet high. As they get close they find a good place to park. It's about two blocks away. They didn't want their cars to be heard rolling up the hill. They need the element of surprise. Not sure that they have it, they creep up towards the house.

As the gang walks up towards the house, it starts to rain a little.

"Just like fuckin' last time," Angelo says.

Yano nods and motions for them to keep moving. As they get close they see a couple of guards on their side of the perimeter wall. Yano sneaks up behind a tree and waits. As the rest of the gang takes cover in some bushes, Yano is twisting a rather large potato onto the barrel of his gun. Yano pops out from behind the tree and puts a bullet in each of the men's heads. The potato, acting as a silencer, started on fire from the heat of the gun powder exploding.

Yano throws the potato to the ground and they all continue towards the wall. It is dark out so climbing over the wall unseen is not a big deal. Easily, they all get over and line up, backs against the wall. Yano whispers to the gang, telling each of them where to go and what to do. Angelo and Vinnie are to cover the back door, the rest of the guys will all cover a window, and Yano and Gino will take the front door. Every escape needs to be properly guarded as to not leave any opens for Don Talapini to slip through this time. Everyone takes their positions and Yano shoots the first bullet. The bullet shatters the front picture window hitting a wall. This was not a shot that was meant to hurt anyone but to tell the rest of his followers to start. As the first bullet pops off, Angelo grabs his cocktail and tosses it at the back door. Flames explode all over the back porch. Men try to run outside but run directly into the flames. Vinnie tosses another one and sets three men on fire. Guards exit the front door and Gino and Yano open fire. As the guards realize that both exits are covered, they all head towards a window. Shooting from every window on both floors, the boys all shoot back.

As the firefight proceeds, Yano makes his way to the front door and enters the house. A man runs down the stairs and Yano quickly puts three bullets in the man's chest. The house is large, there are multiple rooms on the main floor. Yano is inside, killing and exploring before Gino can get in to back him up. Yano walks down the hall slowly, opening door after door. He shoots the men in the rooms as they are shooting at the gang through the windows, completely unaware that Yano is behind them.

Angelo is tossing cocktails at the upper windows as Vinnie unloads his fifty round drum in the Tommy gun. The siding explodes from the house as the bullets tear through it. The flames climbing and finally reaching the roof. Vinnie reloads and starts to dump bullet after bullet at the upper windows and Angelo rushes in through the back door.

Yano bursts into one last room and sees a man sitting at the desk. The man turns his chair around and looks directly at Yano. His face scarred from burns. His hand also scarred. It was Don Talapini. Yano points his gun and looks as if he sees a ghost. Talapini has his gun pointed at Yano.

"So, you came back huh?"

"Did you think I was going to let you continue to terrorize the neighborhood?"

"What took so long?"

"I was otherwise engaged."

"Well do you plan on finishing the job this time?"

"Yes, I do."

Talapini pulls his trigger. A bullet sinks into the flesh of Yano's stomach. Yano is knocked back a step or two and then returns fire. His bullet landing in Talapini's chest. As Talapini fell to the ground, multiple sounds erupt. The background noise of the roof starting to collapse from the fire, a second gunshot, hitting Yano in the shoulder, and a scream from behind. A woman's scream. As Yano turned to see who it was, a third bullet is fired. The girl, holding a pistol of her own, shoots. The bullet that she let fly landing in the side of Yano's neck.

Yano drops his weapon and drops to his knees. Clutching the entrance wound in his neck he looks up at the woman. The two make eye contact and Yano falls to his back. The girl comes over and drops to her knees next to Yano's body. He stares up at her, almost forgetting the fact that he is dying, and smiles. He has been waiting for this day for so long. Arabella drops her pistol and starts crying as she grabs Yano's body. She holds him tight and rocks back and forth. As she looks up, she sees Talapini's lifeless body.

"Daddy?"

She drops Yano and crawls over to Talapini, her father. Already covered in blood and tears she holds her father. Gino finally makes his way into the room, only to see his big brother lying on the floor, dead. He drops his weapon and starts to cry. He looks up and sees Arabella, as he shakes his head he turns back towards Yano. Gino cannot believe what has happened. Gino kneels to sit with his brother. Completely unaware of what is happening, or of the fact that the brothers are even inside, the gang outside continue to send bullets through the windows and siding. Cocktails continue to fly at the house. The roof ablaze, as were the walls. Angelo exits the building.

"I think we got them all, let's get the hell out of here."

Angelo and Vinnie make their way over to the other guys and regroup. They all head towards the front of the house to meet with the brothers, but they are no longer there. They all turn and look back toward the house. Flames tower above the roof now, almost reaching the heavens. Just then, the rest of the roof collapses inwards. As the house begins to sink inwards, the walls buckle. The entire house comes down on top of everyone left inside. There is no way that no one could have survived that. Angelo sends the rest of the guys back to the cars and he waits. He waits and constantly looking back and forth. Searching the yard for any place that the brothers could be hiding. Searching the wreckage of the home, waiting, hoping that they would emerge. Angelo waits for almost thirty minutes before he finally admits to himself what has happened. His eyes swell with tears as he jumps over the wall and rushes to the car. The house collapses the rest of the way.

All pieces of the once tall home, now sitting on the yard, burning. All of Talpaini's men left inside had been burned alive. Don Talapini had been burned alive, along with his daughter, Arabella. The two courageous brothers never made their exit. The Black Hand had finally been dismantled. Angelo collects the guys at the warehouse and pronounces himself the new boss. He proclaims Vinnie to be his second in command, his right hand, his underboss. He names the rest of the men his captains and sends them out to recruit new soldiers. Italians, and Sicilians only. Angelo swore, in the name of the Scarpaccis, that he would detect and destroy every other criminal organization and make neighborhoods all over safe for their citizens to walk the streets again.

About the Author

J. J. Caniglia was born John Joseph Caniglia Jr. Born into an Irish/Sicilian family, he was born and raised on the south side of Omaha Nebraska. He was brought up in a very Sicilian lifestyle where family counts for everything. J. J. is a proud father of four, two girls and two boys. With his wife, Ashleigh, by his side he helped raise four kids while attending Southern New Hampshire University for a bachelor's degree in 3D modeling. When that was finished J. J. immediately went back for a Master's in creative writing. He has been writing stories since he was a young boy and dreams of one day making a living by it.

www.ingramcontent.com/pod-product-compliance
Lightning Source LLC
Chambersburg PA
CBHW032030310726
48972CB00002B/615